WICKED WINGMAN

SAGE SPELLING

Editor: Jennifer Miller
Cover Designer: deliciousnightsdesign.com
Formatted by: Jennifer Eaton

Mom, this one is for you.
Love you!

CHAPTER 1

Buzzed with adrenaline, I flexed my hands around the W-shape of the yoke, and it eased forward.

"Uncle Nas, are we going to land now?" Six-year-old Christopher sat up taller in the copilot seat beside me. Wide-eyed, he clutched the toy aircraft I'd given him when he boarded the plane and peered out the window next to him.

"We sure are, buddy." I relished in my own excitement mirrored through the eyes of a child. It was the same kind of joy I remembered from when I was a kid and had gotten on my first plane.

"This is so cool. I want to be a pilot like you and Uncle Carter when I grow up."

"And you can come work for Fly Kakos with us."

"That would be so awesome," Christopher said.

It was going to be an interesting trip. I don't do family outings, but I couldn't decline when my best friend and business partner, Carter, asked me to fly his family out to Rio for his surprise wedding reception. Besides, who would decline a trip to Rio? The sandy beaches, salty sea air, and the Brazilian food were just a few of the many reasons I loved Rio de Janeiro.

Did I mention the incredible sunsets, the sexy women, the dancing—the women? Yes, I counted women twice. They're worthy of a second and even third mention. So, needless to say, Rio is one of my favorite places to travel, and I couldn't wait to get to the hotel.

"Fly Kakos 979, this is Galeão. Cleared to land, runway two-eight." The brusque, accented voice chirped from my headset, and I squared my shoulders.

My sexy and sleek Bombardier BD-700 luxury plane, Jade, tipped down like a delicate swan. The cockpit quaked with little tremors of turbulence, and my pulse raced.

My insides vibrated. "Cleared to land, runway two-eight, Fly Kakos 979."

Being in the midst of the picturesque sky, airborne between the fluffy white clouds and defying gravity, is an extraordinary sensation, but the touchdown is my greatest high. The windows quivered slightly as we descended and the runway grew closer. My mouth went dry. The wheels descended and my muscles tightened at the *clack* sound. We inclined and glided through the air while I used the yoke to control the approach and carefully eased us to a smooth landing. Gratification rocked through me as the wheels touched the pavement and rolled to a subtle stop.

With a sigh of contentment, I leaned back in the pilot's seat and grabbed the intercom. "Welcome to Rio de Janeiro, Clynes Family."

The cheering from the other side of the door roared over the buzzing sounds of the engine.

"I have to tell my mom that I'm going to be a pilot when I grow up." Christopher unbuckled his seatbelt and headed toward the cockpit door just as someone knocked twice.

Rahim opened the door. His bright blue eyes gleamed with mischief, and he nearly toppled over as Christopher's blond head zoomed past him to the main cabin.

"That's Catherine's boy, right?" Rahim asked. "He and Camille's daughter, Corrine, could pass for twins." He chuckled.

"Yeah, they really could," I said. "Great kids."

"Speaking of twins, you didn't tell me Carter's sisters were fucking hot."

"They're a little too old for you," I warned.

"You know I like experienced women."

"You like them teaching you things, young man?"

"What can I say? I'm a great student." He winked.

Rahim was a handsome devil—tall, dark, and built like a boxer. My little cousin broke hearts everywhere I took him. He'd only been working for me for a few months and had appointed me his mentor. I hadn't minded. I'd taken him under my wing as a favor to my aunt. In truth, I liked the kid. He was smart, driven, and had become a real asset to me at Fly Kakos Airlines in his short time with me.

"Hey, Rahim." The sexy, smooth voice of the elder of the Clynes fraternal twins, Camille, came from behind him. She pressed her sizeable tits against Rahim's back as she peered around him to see me. "Sorry, Captain, I'll have to steal your first mate for a moment."

"First mates are for ships."

"Ships, planes... Seriously, what's the difference?"

"You be careful there, Camille."

She flipped her big blond curls over her shoulder, and her brilliant blue eyes shined with pure trouble. "I promise to take great care of your cousin."

She led Rahim away by his tie, and I chuckled. Her hips swayed above those outrageous red leather heels she'd worn. The poor kid had no idea how badly she was going to chew him up and spit him out, but I had no doubt he'd enjoy every second of that ride.

After getting everyone safely off the plane and through the airport customs, a long and tenuous process, we were finally making our way toward the exit when the endless line of the Clynes family halted, and Camille's voice shrieked with an, "Oh my God!"

Damn it, had we ruined the surprise for Kendall? Carter would kick my ass, but whatever—I couldn't be blamed for that shit. Sighing, I halted behind the Clynes crew with my heart in my throat.

"Holy cannoli, Cammy, Catherine? What are you guys doing here?"

The familiar sweet and cheerful voice was like a knife to the chest. My world tilted. It couldn't be her, but who else would use words like "holy cannoli"? A little light-headed, I swallowed hard.

"You remember my parents," Camille said.

"Of course. It's nice to see you again, Mr. and Mrs. Clynes."

"You too, dear," Mr. Clynes said.

"You will never believe this, but my baby boy Carter is getting married, and we're here for a destination reception," Mrs. Clynes shrieked with delight. She was an older version of Camille and Catherine, but with a more modest appearance and sweeter disposition. I tried to see past her, but she was a lot taller than the person they were speaking to. My pulse quickened.

"Congratulations to all of you. Where are Carter and his blushing bride?"

"They've flown in to meet us." Camille hesitated. "We came in on his friend's plane."

"Camille, this can't be your daughter, Corinne? Oh my goodness, you are just gorgeous, and so much taller than I remember. Are those airplane wings on your shirt?"

Every inch of me wanted to escape, but that sweet voice pulled me forward like a beacon of light.

"Yes, Uncle Nas gave them to me," Corinne said.

"He gave me this airplane too," Christopher said.

"This little one is mine," Catherine said. "He is all about being a pilot like his uncles Carter and Nas."

"Nas?"

Mr. Clynes's broad shoulders shifted in front of me, and before I could run for it, big brown eyes blazed into mine. My heart stopped beating.

"Naseem?" Her purse fell from her hands. Papers and all kinds of little metal things scattered the terminal floor.

All at once, everyone scrambled to collect her belongings, but she and I just gawped at one another. An older and more sophisticated, but still absolutely fucking gorgeous, Summer Seba stood, eyes wide, openmouthed, and sporting the same shell-shocked expression that mirrored my own out-of-body experience. Her faultless heart-shaped face froze, those perfect red, plump lips parted and quivered. It was like time stood still and our greatest hits hit me like a ton of bricks. My brain wouldn't connect with my mouth, and it took a few moments before I found coherent words.

"What are you doing here?" My voice sounded foreign even to my own ears.

She closed her eyes, and after five heartbeats, a more calm and indifferent woman ignored me. With a deliberate eye roll, she brushed away the dark, lush hair from her face and bent down to help retrieve her things.

Her complete dismissal of me awakened me from my shock. My stomach hardened and I balled my fists to my sides. Time really did change people, because the girl I knew in high school would never be so disrespectful to ignore anyone.

"What a small world." Camille handed Summer a hairbrush and some sort of compact. "Where are you headed?"

"I was supposed to be in Argentina, but we had plane trouble, and now I'm stuck in Rio until tomorrow morning. Since there aren't any commercial flights or hotel rooms at the airport available, I was just about to see if I could charter a plane instead of waiting for my rescheduled flight," Summer said.

"You should totally come to Maria Rosa's with us," Camille said.

"Who's Maria Rosa?" I asked.

"The villa we're renting while we're here. I thought you knew where we were going?" Camille glared at me.

What the devil was going on, and what happened to staying at a nice private hotel? I had not planned on spending all week in a villa with the Brady Bunch. How was I supposed to take women back to my room if there were kids around? Besides, were they really inviting Summer there now too? Did Camille hate me that much? What the fuck was wrong with her?

"No, I'm okay." Summer glanced at me from the corner of her eye.

"You shouldn't be stuck here all by yourself for twenty-four hours, or pay the extra expense for a charter plane," Camille said. "Come back with us. You can bunk with me—it'll be like that time in Spain."

"I don't want to intrude. You're here for a wedding reception."

"Don't be silly. Besides, I'm dying to hear what you've been up to all this time."

"And it's not safe for a young lady like yourself. Is it, Naseem?" It was Mrs. Clynes's turn to glare at me.

"No, it's not safe." I was conflicted between duty and dread. Summer Seba was standing in front of me after twelve years of me burying memories of her, along with the rest of my tormented past, but it wasn't safe for her to be on her own overnight in a foreign airport. "I'll call and reserve you a room at Rio Love."

"She's coming with us." Camille's scowl was getting deadlier by the second.

How could I stay in the same house with Summer fucking Seba? I'd have to get everyone settled because I promised Carter, but after that, I was out. I'd reserve myself a room at Rio Love, and maybe a fucking massage too. I was going to need it.

"My brother reserved us this adorable villa where he and his fiancée first spent a weekend together... It's a crazy story," Camille said. "I'll have to tell you over drinks."

"Bus is here." With all the commotion, I'd forgotten Rahim was with us.

"Good, let's roll, people. I'm dying to put my toes in

the sand." Camille trudged toward the door, arm in arm with Summer and clutching Corrine's hand.

Fuck. Fuck. *Fuck.* I loosened my tie and started after them, shell-shocked. Someone in the heavens was playing a sick joke on me. I half expected Ashton Kutcher to jump out and yell, "You've been punk'd!"

Carter had ordered a limo bus to accommodate all of us, and I made the awkward walk to the completely opposite end of the bus from Summer with an interested Rahim on my heels.

"Who is that hottie?" Rahim asked.

"Off-limits."

"Wow, she must be someone special because you've never said that before."

"Can it, Rahim."

"Bro, you loved her."

"Keep your fucking voice down."

"Yo, you don't have a game face. You should have seen your expression when you saw her. You looked like you jumped off a plane and your parachute didn't open."

"It's complicated."

"Like the social media status." He chuckled.

"See if you can get us rooms at the Rio Love. I can't stay in that house with her." I heard the desperation in my own voice.

"I got you." Rahim started tapping on his phone, all humor gone from his tone.

There was a time that girl had been everything—my high school love, my best friend, the girl I pictured forever with—but life happened and changed me. My entire life course was altered forever.

The limo bus was lined with soft black leather seats that wrapped around the entirety of the interior like a living room sectional sofa. Flashing blue neon lights and dark cherrywood trimmed all the tinted windows on either side of the space, and there was a minibar, but unfortunately, it was only stocked with soft drinks. Lord knew I could've really used a drink after being confronted with this blast from the past.

I attempted to avert my gaze but couldn't take my eyes off of Summer. I watched her sitting cross-legged diagonally from me—her thick, delicious thighs, little black shorts, and those sexy ankle-strapped wicker shoes with the funny-shaped heels women always seem to wear on vacation.

Our stares met, and a glimmer of pain shone through her big brown eyes. The memory of the last time we saw each other slammed into me like a runaway train. The grief in my heart, the pain in her eyes, the hurtful things I'd said to get her to go to Spain without me echoed inside my mind. She quickly averted her stare, but I could have sworn she'd remembered it all too. I watched her close her eyes and do that breathing thing again.

One. Two. Three. Four. Five. Her eyes fluttered open just like before. She'd used the moment to gather her emotions, and now all sentiments were completely blank from her beautiful face. She gave me an indifferent glance before she looked away and started chatting with Catherine, and I was trapped in the memories of my high school greatest hits.

"We have two rooms reserved," Rahim whispered.

"Good."

HOLY FRITTERS! NASEEM KAKOS HAD BEEN GOOD-looking as a teenager, but holy cannoli, the guy in front of me was hotter than fish grease. The same wavy black hair and hypnotizing dark eyes, but in a new-and-improved 2.0 version with a mysterious dark façade and chiseled everything from jaw to calves. *Just look at how his black slacks cling to his muscular legs. Oh fudge, we aren't going down that train of thought.* No way, no how.

What were the odds? In twelve years, I never once bumped into him in West Bloomfield, where we grew up, or anywhere else in Michigan. I hadn't seen him since high school, and I just happened to bump into him in an airport when I'm on my way to meet my future husband? Someone up in Heaven was having a great laugh at my expense. Probably my grams, bless her soul. My maternal grandmother was against arranged marriages, and I could totally see her messing with my luck just so I wouldn't go through with it. But seeing Naseem, remembering the state he left me in the night before we were supposed to leave for Spain, was just the confirmation I needed that I was doing absolutely the right thing.

"So what's in Argentina?" Another beauty just like her twin sister, Camille, Catherine was a stunner—big blue eyes, salon-ready blond hair styled to perfection, and a demeanor to match. She was the perfect combination of cute and sexy that I always strove for but seemed to never get right.

"I'm getting married."

"What? Oh my God, how exciting! Congratulations. Cammy, did you hear, Summer is getting married. We should totally do a batch party tonight to celebrate."

Maybe I should have kept that little nugget to myself.

I glanced at Naseem, and when our eyes met, an electric current radiated through me.

"Who's the lucky guy? Where is he? Are you doing a destination thing?"

Between Camille and Catherine's questions, I was starting to hyperventilate. *One. Two. Three. Four. Five.* Heat sizzled up my body and danced at my spine. My face burned.

"I, ahh, well, his name is Laith, and he lives in Argentina," I said.

"The foreign exchange student, Laith?" Naseem's voice caught me completely off guard. I hadn't realized that he was still paying attention to me, and the stunned look in his eyes perplexed me.

"You remember him?"

"How could I not? He followed you around all semester when he was in school with us."

"Our families are friends. I was the only person he knew."

"He followed you around like a lapdog."

"Oh, how cute," Catherine said.

"Oh, I remember him. He was the boy that took the detour home just so he could spend a few days with us in Spain," Camille said.

I laughed. "Yes, he insisted that he show us his favorite restaurants before we parted."

"Seriously, you guys have stayed in touch all this time?" Camille said.

"Yes." Technically, it wasn't a complete lie, but I couldn't admit that I hadn't seen anything but a few pictures of him and we'd only had a few social media chats before I'd agreed to marry him.

"I don't see a ring," Naseem said from his corner of the bus.

I rolled my eyes. "We're picking one out when I get there. He did send me this lovely betrothal gift." I flashed him my diamond tennis bracelet.

"That's stunning," Catherine said.

"Gorgeous," Camille said. "The man always had good taste."

She winked at me and glared at Naseem. If her eyes could shoot daggers, I'm pretty sure he'd have a few knives penetrating his skin. If Camille was anything, she was a total mama bear with everyone she loved, and I was lucky to be in that small circle. She'd been one of the few people that had seen my breakdown because she was the one who'd found me after he shattered my heart. We had been virtual strangers, but she'd quickly become someone I'd been able to lean on. Being a couple years older, she'd understood my devastation, and I honestly don't know how I would've gone through those gut-wrenching moments without her.

"Yeah, excellent."

The condescending tone in Naseem's voice was a slap in the face.

"Yeah, some of us didn't know better when were younger. But he always seemed to be intelligent and recognized true beauty," I said.

"Seriously, you're so right. The boys we dated in high school are still dickheads," Camille said.

"You still only date the wrong men," Catherine mumbled for only Camille and me.

One point for each twin—these girls were on a roll today. I suppressed a giggle and chanced a glance at Naseem's brooding form. Our eyes met, and heat radiated from his glower. He had the nerve to be angry with me, seriously? I glared back with the same fury in my stare. My heart raced and my stomach knotted, but I wasn't going to back down—never again from him.

When I'd agreed to join them overnight, I wasn't planning on even noting his presence, but he'd inserted himself into our conversation and acted like a jerk because he didn't approve of my choices. What did he think would happen, I'd just forgive and forget? I would never forget those words he'd said to me—they were the fuel behind my ten-year plan, my drive for success, the reason I couldn't give my love freely and had opted for an arranged marriage. He'd ruined a bright-eyed girl with passion, an open heart, and wild childhood dreams—and left this broken shell of a person he was currently looking down on. I lifted my chin and squared my shoulders. *Fudge you, Naseem Kakos. You will never have any power over me again.*

CHAPTER 2

The ride from the airport was a fucking bitch and I nearly kissed the ground when we finally arrived at Maria Rosa's villa. It was actually a lot nicer than I thought, but it wasn't the Rio Love. Once the Clynes bunch were all settled in, Rahim and I would be off on our next adventure at the luxury pool, and we wouldn't have to report back here for a few days for the reception—when Summer fucking Seba was on her fucking way to marry Laith. Seriously, Laith? Out of all people, she decided to marry him? He was a backstabbing dick who did anything he could to come between me and Summer—including snitching to her brother about us.

Taking Mrs. Clynes's bags along with my own, I followed her up the grand front steps that were framed between a set of white Greek empire-type columns. Flower baskets of all sorts lined a wraparound patio. The double white doors opened, and Carter appeared.

"You're here," Mrs. Clynes shouted.

"Keep it down. Kendall doesn't know you guys are

coming, remember?" Carter wrapped his mother in a bear hug, and my heart clenched with a little bit of envy.

"My married boy."

He laughed and kissed her forehead. "Let me help you there, bud." Carter took one of the bags from me, and we fist-bumped because our hands were filled with luggage. "Thanks for bringing out my family—I really appreciate it."

"They're my family, they just humor you." I laughed.

Carter chuckled. "Are you ready to be my best man?"

"Best man? I thought this was just a reception."

"Yeah, you'll still need to give a speech."

"I can handle that," I said.

"Is there any way you would consider renewing your vows with us? It would make me so happy to see you, my only son, pledge your love to Kendall," Mrs. Clynes said.

I glanced at Carter, and he gave me a defeated look. "I'll check with my wife. If she wants to, I'll hire a minister when we go out for groceries."

"We?"

Carter sighed. "Best man, my friend. That's part of the responsibilities."

My stomach tightened. My dream of sneaking away wasn't going to be as easy as I thought. I glanced toward Rahim, but he was busy flirting with Camille and Catherine while he helped them with their bags. Somehow, I didn't think the motherfucker would mind staying. I, on the other hand, needed to escape Summer the moment I had the chance. Maybe after the grocery run, Carter would release me from my best man duties for the night.

I shrugged. "I mean, if you're stupid enough to get

married, at the very least, I have to be there to witness your death sentence."

"Oh, is that what marriage is to you, a death sentence?" Summer was standing behind me with Camille and Catherine in tow.

The shock of Carter's face mirrored my own. He glanced at me and then at her. "Summer?"

"Sorry for crashing your party." Summer had taken off her blazer and her sheer tank clung to every scrumptious curve of her breasts.

"I invited her to stay with us. The poor girl was stranded at the airport, and I knew you wouldn't mind," Camille said.

"Of course not, I'm happy you could be here." Carter reached out and hugged Summer, but his apologetic stare found mine. I read the "what the fuck?" written on his expression, and it totally matched my current mood. We made our way inside the villa, and Carter showed us to the sitting area while he went to get Kendall for the surprise.

The room was filled with bulky, mismatched furniture—from large orange sofas to white and flowery chairs. Tall white bookshelves framed a white mantel and fireplace. Rahim and I finished bringing in the rest of the luggage and found a couple empty chairs in the corner of the room.

"Look at the monkey, Mama." Christopher pointed over my shoulder.

I looked up to find a tiny grey monkey sitting on the back of my chair. "Hi, little guy, you're a handsome one."

The monkey smiled and trotted over to sit on my shoulder. "What's his name?" I asked.

"I don't know, but Uncle Carter told me about him," Christopher said.

I felt something warm and wet on my back. I squirmed, praying it wasn't what I thought it was, just as the monkey leaped off my shoulder and disappeared from sight. I stood, warm liquid poured down my spine, and I writhed.

"He told me he likes to pee on new people." Christopher giggled.

"Looks like he struck again," Camille said.

Gagging, I tugged off my shirt, balled it up, and looked for a garbage can. "I liked this shirt."

"Well, if it's any consolation, you look better without it." Camille winked.

"Oh my God. What are you guys doing here?" Kendall stopped short in the doorway with Carter on her heels, lunged inside the living room, and grabbed a hold of Carter's mom. "I'm so happy you're here."

Kendall had Hollywood beauty, and I could never get over how much she resembled a young Michelle Pfeiffer —she could be her doppelganger from the movie *Scarface.*

"Oh honey, don't cry. We are so excited to share this with you," Mrs. Clynes said.

Carter eased around the rest of the Clynes greeting Kendall. "Well, I see you didn't waste any time getting undressed."

"That damn monkey peed on me."

"I wondered who would be its next victim." Carter laughed.

"Victim, what victim?" Kendall had made her way over to Rahim and had her arms around him.

"The monkey just got him," Carter said.

"Oh, that's why you have all that man chest exposed."

Kendall laughed. "I'll wait to give you a proper greeting later. Maybe after you get the pee off of you."

"Yeah, I need to clean up before the grocery run. Where's the bathroom?" I said.

"You have time for a shower and change before we go. Maria Rosa isn't back with the jeep yet," Carter said.

"No, I'll shower at the hotel after the food run." I was testing the waters. If Carter didn't freak, we would be free and clear to leave later. He had to know that staying under the same roof as Summer Seba was completely out of the question for me.

"Where do you think you're going?" Carter said.

"We have rooms reserved at Rio Love," Rahim said.

"Cancel them. I have rooms reserved for you guys here."

"Yes, you can't leave." Camille had sauntered over, and her focus was on poor Rahim. "I was hoping we could all hang at the beach."

Rahim didn't seem to mind one bit, and I could've sworn I heard Carter mumble something like, "The poor kid doesn't know what web he's fallen into," because Kendall laughed, and Camille gave him one of her lethal stares before turning away and approaching Summer, who'd somehow gotten herself cross-legged and was playing some electronic game with Christopher and Corinne on the floor.

"Come with me, roomie. Let's go get our suits on," Camille said. "Hey jerk-face, does it matter which room?"

"Nope. The entire villa is ours for the week, so just claim a room," Carter said.

"I was wondering why the place was empty. I'll show you around." Kendall went to join the others.

While I watched them go, Carter punched me in the arm. "How the fuck did that happen?"

"Don't know. Someone was playing a cruel joke on me."

"'Across the Universe'?"

"Another Beatles title, right?" I rolled my eyes.

"It fucking fits. Are you okay?"

"Yeah, why wouldn't I be?"

I dead-ass lied to my best friend. Every fiber of my being was on fire. My emotions were scrambled. How could I be happy, sad, terrified, and confused all at the same time? Seeing her stirred up so many memories, and not just ones that reminded me of her. Her presence was a symbol of everything I'd lost since we were a couple, and everything that we could've had if we'd stayed together.

"So is someone going to tell me who this girl is?" Rahim's voice broke into my thoughts.

"She's the one girl our boy ever loved."

"What? Mr. Worldwide, I-don't-do-relationships was in love once upon a time?"

"More than in love. He loved her enough to let her go," Carter said.

"I don't get it," Rahim said.

"That's what I said all that time ago. Maybe I'll understand it now if you explained it, Nas," Carter said.

"Shut it, both of you."

"Seriously, if Camille"—Rahim earmuffed Carter—"turns me down, you wouldn't mind me giving her a holler?"

"She's engaged," I warned. Anger raged through me, and I wasn't sure if it was her being engaged to that *ufftie*

Laith or Rahim's jab at hitting it with my ex that pissed me off more.

"Bro, I'll be a last fling. Chicks do that shit all the time before they tie the knot."

"Not all chicks." Carter glared.

"No, Kendall is excluded from this." Rahim put both his hands up in surrender. Then he turned his stare on me. "You wouldn't mind if I hit that?"

"I will fucking kill you," I snapped. I walked away, looking for an available bedroom so I could shower this monkey piss off of me, but I still heard Carter and Rahim cackling like a couple of teenage girls.

Rahim's voice echoed behind me. "Guess I'm canceling the room reservations."

~

"Thank you so much for letting me crash with you. I can't imagine still sitting in the airport."

"Of course, I couldn't leave you stranded there. I should have, though." Camille tossed a blue throw pillow at my head, and I ducked.

"Hey, what's that for?"

Camille sat cross-legged on the plush, fluffy white bed while I sat on the brightest blue chair I'd ever seen and untied the laces on my wedges while avoiding her stare.

"That's for being MIA for months."

"My ankles are swollen." I attempted to steer the conversation. "I probably ate too much salt on the plane."

"Sit and put your feet up." Camille moved over on the bed and made room for me. "Then you can tell me why you dropped off the face of the earth."

"I didn't."

"You did. When was the last time I saw you?" She was on her knees on the bed with both hands on her hips staring down at me. "Like, last year after the New York Wine and Food Festival?"

"I've been busy. The job had me living out of my suitcase."

"Seriously, you're going to use that excuse with me?"

I sighed and fell onto the bed beside her. "No, I'm sorry."

She was absolutely right. I had pushed away everyone around me because the deadline of my ten-year plan was approaching, and I'd essentially agreed to basically marrying a stranger. My American-born friends would never understand my reasons for doing it and not waiting for true love.

"So dish. What's going on with you?"

"I got wrapped up in work, but I am sorry. I missed you." I wrapped my arms around her torso and squeezed, then lost whatever energy I'd conserved and fell back on the pillow.

"You will have to find a way to make it up to me. Maybe a double date with Nas and Rahim? Show the asshole what he missed out on all those years ago."

"You know that is definitely not happening."

"Right, because you're engaged?"

"I'm engaged and I hate Naseem."

"You never found out why he all of a sudden changed his mind the day before we left for Spain?"

"He made his reasons quite clear when he dumped me."

Camille gave me a questioning stare and rested on the bed beside me. "Okay, but don't you think it's strange that you got stranded on your way to get married and then bumped into all of us?"

"No, it's just a wicked coincidence. Besides, maybe I was meant to bump into you."

"So you could be my wingman with Rahim?"

I laughed. "I'll be your wingman, but you will have to be my buffer with Naseem. I can't be left alone with him."

"Deal. But seriously, isn't Rahim hot?"

"Isn't Rahim like ten years younger than you?"

"Seven, and he will have just the right amount of stamina to keep me satisfied."

"You're a dirty bird." I laughed.

"Which reminds me, you're fucking getting married. You and Laith? How did that happen?"

My stomach sank. "It, umm, kind of just happened."

"Seriously? You never mentioned keeping in contact with him."

"Well, I...umm, we... Fudge. I just can't lie to you."

"I knew it, you're not getting married. I can't believe I fell for that one. You and Laith, how ridiculous."

"I *am* getting married to Laith, but we only fell back in contact with each other a few weeks ago, after our families arranged our marriage. Apparently, our parents are investing in a hotel chain in Jordan together."

"Seriously? So you're a pawn in your family's business deal?"

"No. Yes... I don't know. The proposal came along with the news of the investment. But it doesn't matter. I'm agreeing to marry Laith because I want to."

I took the pillow from under my head and smothered my face. Right here, this conversation was everything I didn't need right now. I knew what Camille was going to say, that I shouldn't get married if it wasn't for love.

She pulled the pillow away from my face. "Look at me. I swear I feel like I'm dealing with Corinne right now."

I groaned and stared into her crystal blue eyes. "I know what you're going to say."

"Is this about your ten-year plan?"

"You don't understand."

"I understand, more than you know. Remember, I got pregnant from a one-night stand and turned down Corinne's dad's marriage proposal."

"We are not the same. You want love and all that happily-ever-after crap. I don't. I want an arrangement, not a love affair."

Camille dropped the pillow back on my face and let out the loudest sigh. "You're still the same stubborn ass you were at eighteen."

"Are you done, Mother, because I'd really like to get a drink or ten," I said.

"Now this, I could totally get with."

After quick showers, we got in our suits and headed to the kitchen to find Kendall and Catherine already getting a pitcher of margaritas ready.

"Yes, liquor. We need lots of it," Camille ordered. "Where are the kiddos?"

"Mom and Dad took them to the beach and have given us full permission to get hammered tonight."

"Here you go, ladies." Kendall placed two nice-size margarita glasses in front of Camille and me. I didn't hesitate to take a large gulp of the sweet and tart goodness. It burned in a mouthwatering way in my gut, and heat washed over me.

"Good and strong."

"Oh, that reminds me, where is my handsome pilot

trainee?" Camille asked.

"Easy, Stella." I laughed.

"Oh, honey, I never lost my groove."

Camille hit a few buttons on her phone and old-school freestyle music blared from the little speaker on the kitchen counter.

"Oh, Lord." Catherine covered her eyes. "I never understood what appealed to you about this eighties and nineties music."

Camille, on the other hand, was shaking her hips like this was a 2000s dance-off and singing along with Lil Suzy's "Real Love." Something about the lyrics shook me extra hard today. While Lil Suzy sang about real love being about fun and games and about the man that broke her heart, I felt the music down into the deepest part of my soul. Still raw from my encounter with the man who had done that to me just today, anger ripped through me, and I sang along with Camille like I was Mariah Carey putting on a concert.

"Was it me, or did that song feel like we were venting?" Camille asked.

I rolled my eyes and downed the rest of my margarita.

"Looks like someone needs a refill." Camille filled my glass. "You know what I miss...those cookies you used to make—that was your grandmother's recipe."

"Oh, the sugar ones?"

"Yes, they used to melt in my mouth."

"I can make them. It's just butter, sugar, and flour."

"Yes. Now. Kendall, do you think we can ask Maria Rosa for those ingredients?"

"Yes, I'm sure she won't mind," Kendall said.

Sure enough, Kendall returned with all we needed, and I started to make us cookies. My paternal grandmother, Nana, had taught me everything I knew about cooking Middle Eastern cuisine. When was the last time I'd made any of her recipes, or even been in a kitchen actually making something myself? As I kneaded the dough, I realized it had been a long time—since my promotion. Somehow, between the traveling and the development of exclusive hotels around the world, I'd stopped actually doing any cooking myself. My job was to create the environment, put the right people in place to keep the vision going, and move on to the next adventure.

The song changed, and Cynthia's voice blared through the speakers, singing about being held in her lover's arms, him telling her he loved her, and all the air left my lungs. I'd blocked this memory out of my mind, but just like unwanted rain on a sunny day, memories of me in Naseem's parents' kitchen flooded my mind.

"Change the track, please," I tried to say, but for some reason, I couldn't get my voice over a whisper, and with Camille singing and now having Catherine join, they couldn't hear me.

"Honey, I'm home." Carter's voice broke into the craziness. He and Naseem entered carrying four shopping bags each.

A sequence of, "What did you bring," "Finally, I'm hungry," and "Seriously, it's about time," resonated through the kitchen, but all I saw was Naseem. The empty baking dish I was holding nearly tumbled from my fingertips while I stood trapped in one of the many memories I'd suppressed deep inside my tattered heart. He was watching Catherine holding a banana in her hand as a microphone and doing a very convincing Johnny. His gaze turned toward me, and our eyes met. Shock flickered in his stare, and I knew he remembered that day as well.

CHAPTER 3

Carter had me running my ass all over fucking Rio with a laundry list of shit that wouldn't have been necessary if we'd just stayed at Rio Love or any other fucking hotel.

"Tell me again, so I can understand why we are staying at this godforsaken villa where we have to fetch stuff like food and drinks?"

"Well, Maria Rosa would have gotten everything, but I feel like it would have been too much for her."

"I understand that, but why here and not at a hotel… you know, with room service?"

"Because it's a special place for me and my girl, and I really didn't want to get married at a place I'd take women to get laid."

I rolled my eyes. "When did you become so pussy-whipped?"

"Honestly, from the moment I walked into that airport bar and saw her sitting there."

"You don't even deny it."

"Nope." He tossed two bags of groceries at me and

headed toward the front door.

"You're a proud pussy. I fucking love it."

"I do recall a certain curvy brunette that had your tighty whities all twisted back in the day. I'd say you know the sentiment well because you've been pretty pussy-whipped yourself."

"I was a kid."

"And seeing her doesn't make all those feelings come back?" Carter asked.

"No." I said that too quickly to be plausible, even to myself.

Carter reached for the door handle. "Right." He chuckled. "For some reason, I don't believe you."

"Shut the fuck up and get the door." I rolled my eyes.

Carter laughed and opened the way in, and I followed him into the kitchen but stopped short at the scene before us.

It was like I was having an out-of-body experience. My heart raced, my palms were sweaty, and my fingers trembled. The sight we'd walked in on took me back to when I was sixteen years old. Summer was wearing a sexy bikini top with those triangles that just barely covered her big boobs and a flirty, short skirt that was completely see-through down to her red bikini bottoms. But what got me traveling through time was the sight of her in the kitchen and the lyrics to "Dream Boy Dream Girl," by Johnny O and Cynthia.

She used to cook for me almost every day during my last year in high school. Since my parents worked twelve to fifteen hours a day at our family's supermarket, my house was basically a parent-free zone. My brother had already gone off to college, so it was just me and Summer playing house.

But that song was the reason I'd finally gotten a home run. Up until then, Summer wouldn't let me get past third base. She'd let me hot dog her, but of course, that's technically not sex because there wasn't any actual entry.

Summer had loved to sing and dance while cooking. It was one of the many reasons I loved watching her cook. She always sang the lyrics to me, especially the female lines. But one day, I decided to sing to her instead, and the look on her face was fucking priceless.

She was standing at my stove and stirring the pot to one of the newest recipes she'd gotten from watching the Food Channel. But what had me hypnotized was how sexy she looked in my baseball jersey. This particular jersey had shrunk in the wash, and the shirt was barely covering her round ass. I loved seeing my name written across her back, claiming her and that sexy ass as mine.

"Want a taste?" She'd raised her spoon for me to come over.

"Of you, yes. All day."

"You're so dirty."

"Absolutely."

She shook her head and brought the spoon to her own lips instead. "Your loss. This is scrumptious."

"I bet you taste better."

She rolled her eyes, but amusement danced behind her pout.

The new DJ Kal's mix CD played, and I knew the tracks by heart from the number of times she'd already played the CD. DJ Kal was a local Detroit celebrity who was pretty popular for his freestyle mixed CDs, and Summer loved freestyle. "Dream Boy Dream Girl" was on the deck next. I waited patiently as the song changed and Cynthia's voice echoed through the kitchen talking about the first time Johnny told her he loved her. For some reason, Summer hadn't danced toward me like she'd done a million times before, but she sang along and even glanced my way a few times.

Then it was Johnny's turn to sing, and I seized the opportunity. I sounded horrible—I was sure of it—but the delight in her voice was worth every moment of my embarrassing awkward dance moves and shrieking voice. I sang my heart along with Johnny and confessed how lucky I was to have her in my life, and how I wouldn't ever let her go. Out of breath, laughing, and completely horny, we'd completed the duet, and she'd led me to my bedroom where she'd given herself to me.

For some reason, kissing her that time was different. It was soft, slow, and romantic. All the other times it always seemed frantic, like I couldn't get enough of her and she of me. But this time, I wanted to remember every moment of this day. I was so fucking in love with this girl and I felt even more amazing because she'd chosen me to be her first and I hoped she'd be my last because I couldn't picture anyone else in my future.

"I've loved you since kindergarten," I'd whispered. "I'll love you forever."

She'd cupped my face, and we took our relationship to the next level. She'd wrapped her legs around my waist, and I'd slowly made love to my dream girl for the very first time.

~

"SERIOUSLY, YOU GAVE UP THE GOODS FOR A freestyle song?" Camille snagged Cat's margarita and took a sip.

"You've done it for less. And get your own drink." Cat snatched her drink back from her sister. Cat seemed as liberated as I felt. She wobbled and fell back into her own tanning chair, splashing margarita down her chest. "I think that's an adorable story."

"What is in this drink? Truth serum?" I couldn't believe I'd just shared that story with them. My heart was raw, and the emotions I'd worked so hard to forget were raging through me. I'd barely even spoken to him, but since the moment I'd laid eyes on him at the airport, I'd become a complete mess.

"Seriously, whatever it is, I want more." She reached for Cat's drink, and Cat reluctantly shared with her twin.

I could see Naseem from the other side of the patio, and acid burned in my throat. The margaritas I'd drunk on an empty stomach threatened to come up. I quickly stood from my seat, and my legs wobbled.

"What's with you? You look green."

"I'm fine, just need a walk to clear my head."

"Want me to come along?" Cat offered.

"No, stay and enjoy the mommy-free time."

Walking on the white sand was proving to be more difficult than I'd anticipated. Holy fudge cakes, I was more intoxicated than I'd realized, but it was too late to turn back. I made my way to the ocean, the salty sea breeze on my face, working to clear the fog from my mind. How could this actually be happening to me right now? I'd traveled all over the world because of my new job and, even before that, I'd traveled all over Europe, working with chefs, and I'd never once bumped into him. We were from the same hometown, basically attended the same Catholic church, but never once after I left did I even hear his name. Never once had he ever wandered into a restaurant I was running, or working as head chef for, or opening. But here, on my way to marry a man that Naseem had warned me away from in high school, I bump into him. Naseem Kakos.

Somehow, I made it to the shore, and I let the cool, wild waves splash and wade around my toes. The smooth sand swallowing my feet, I took a few more steps in the amazing ocean. The water was now just above my waist. The sounds of the waves and the call of the birds hypnotized me.

Something moved against my toes in the water and I yelped. I lost my balance, and my head went under. Salt covered my tongue and burned my eyes. I struggled to stand, but something was attacking my legs, and as much as I kicked my feet, I couldn't get it off me. I was going to die—something was either going to eat me or I was going to drown. I swallowed another mouthful of saltwater just as a beast grabbed me around the waist. Fighting against the monster's hold, somehow, I was lifted out of the water. I swung wildly but was trapped beneath hard muscle.

"Fuck. Summer, are you okay?"

Naseem's voice was both a relief and dreaded. He moved my hair off my face and dark-as-night eyes stared deeply into my own and assessed.

"Something"—I coughed—"was eating my ankles." A full-on coughing fit started, and I struggled to breathe. God, why was this happening to me? And out of everyone in the house and on this beach, did it have to be him to save me? He attempted to lead me to the shoreline, but something was pulling me back under. Naseem caught me, again. Fudge. This time, he lifted me up and carried me out of the water. Humiliated and completely deflated, I stopped fighting him.

He set me down in the warm sun, and I fell back on the sand. My chest burned and heaved, and thank God, the coughing finally subsided.

"Am I bleeding? I have to be bleeding from whatever was eating my ankles."

"No. No blood anywhere that I can see."

"Thanks for helping me."

Naseem was sitting next to me in the sand, his gorgeous face smirking at me. "Want to know what was eating your ankles?"

"It must have been a big giant fish."

"It was this." He lifted up a large piece of slimy seaweed. "This was what was wrapped around your ankles."

"Well, bacon and a biscuit, I almost drowned because of seaweed." I closed my eyes to hide my shame.

"You still swear using food words?" He laughed.

No, you don't. Nope. You don't get to ask me questions like you know me. That pathetic, lovesick girl doesn't live here anymore.

"Why did you follow me, anyway?" *Why does he look so mouthwatering without a shirt?* My eyes wandered on their own accord over his muscular forearms, chiseled stomach, and that wondrous happy trail.

"I saw you wobbling down here and thought we should talk because it looks like we will be hanging around each other tonight."

"Talk about what?" *Thank you for the reminder that he was the snake and his body was the forbidden apple.*

"How we left things."

"That was a long time ago. It doesn't matter anymore."

"Right, I forgot, because you're getting married?"

There was bitterness in his tone, and it confused the hell out of me.

I sat up. The world went a little tipsy, but I steeled myself and squared my shoulders. "We are here because of mutual friends. That's all."

"That's it?"

"What else is there to say?" *My life exploded the moment you turned your back on me? That the reason that Camille and I are so close, even though she's a few years older, is because she found me at the back of the school, my heart shattered into a million pieces?*

He sighed. "I think I owe you an explanation."

Oh no, not now. I couldn't deal with this. Too many emotions that I worked so hard to toss in the wastebasket were clouding my brain. Along with the margaritas and the near-death experience. None of it was helping to keep my guard up.

I somehow found the strength—maybe it was adrenaline coursing through my veins, or maybe it was just pure terror, but my legs found their footing, and I stood and glared down at him.

"No, I don't need an explanation. It was a lifetime ago. Thank you for saving me from"—I hesitated—"the seaweed."

I did the best I could to make it back to the house without bobbing on my feet, and it almost worked until I lost my footing, again, and face-planted in the sand. I heard Naseem snicker behind me, and fury coursed through me. He must have followed me back to the house.

I glared over my shoulder. "Fudge off, Kakos."

I was done. No more drinking, at least for the rest of the afternoon.

"We're about to eat. Your girl and Cammy made us dinner." Carter collapsed into the chair beside me.

"She's not my girl, and stop giving me shit." I took another drag of my drink, but I was too intoxicated to feel the burn of the amber liquor.

"She could be, if you stopped being a jackass and told her the real reason why you broke up with her."

I shook my head. "I tried talking to her, but she didn't even give me a chance to apologize, even after I saved her drunk ass from drowning."

"It was a good thing you followed her, or this wouldn't have been funny." Carter laughed.

"Man, ever since I saw her head go under the wave and not come up, I..." My words burned in my throat.

"You still love her."

"No, I just can't shake the thought of what could have happened if I hadn't followed her to talk." I turned to face Carter. "What if she'd drowned?"

"You can't think like that. She's fine. You were there and pulled her out."

"I know." I covered my face with my trembling hands. "Fuck."

"Well, did you talk to her?"

"No. I tried, but that stubborn, hard-headed girl wouldn't give me a chance. Maybe she's so whipped over Laith that she doesn't want to hear my explanation." The guy's name was bitter on my tongue.

"Who is he? Should I remember him?"

"Do you remember the foreign exchange student?"

"The asshat that told George you guys were dating?"

"Yup."

"You got your ass whipped because of that motherfucker, now he gets the girl?" Carter chuckled. "He thought that was going to force you to break up."

"Yeah, but he was really shook when George and Nash took her and I to school the next day." My laugh was bitter to my own ears.

"What did you tell George that day? I was sure he was going to kill you, but he just stopped." Carter took a pull of his drink. "And helped you off the floor."

I closed my eyes and remembered the sting of George's fist against my jaw. I'd been pinned to the ground, and I'd let him hit me. After a few good right hooks to my face, George pulled back but still had me pinned beneath him. He'd been surprised that I wasn't protecting myself from his punches and complicated his plans of a fair-ass beating. I could still remember his weary voice when he asked, "Why aren't you fighting me back?"

"I told him I knew I wasn't good enough for her, but I would try every day to be a better man for her."

"Well, you stood by your word." Carter rolled his eyes. "Come on, let's get some dinner."

I sighed. "I'll be there in a minute."

Carter placed his heavy palm on my shoulder. "Brother, you are good enough—you're the only one that doesn't see it."

I downed the rest of my drink and considered Carter's words. Maybe I was better than I believed, but that still didn't change the fact that I was fighting against a ticking time bomb that would invariably ruin the life of anyone who planned a future with me.

CHAPTER 4

Someone must have ignited my abdomen with a blazing fire that moved through my torso and up my esophagus. Acid followed the burn and my stomach groaned. I lurched from the bed and stumbled toward the bathroom. Just barely making it to the toilet, I fell to my knees.

After heaving things I didn't even remember eating, there was an insistent buzzing in my ears, and it just wouldn't stop. It was like the little drummer was inside my head beating his drum to a Metallica song.

I washed my face and brushed my teeth, then I wobbled back in the bedroom to find the thing that had been poking me in the side was probably Catherine's foot. Camille was not in bed, and I was betting she'd shagged Rahim.

The sun was blaring and illuminating the entire bedroom with sunshine, burning my eyes. My phone was MIA, but I found Catherine's phone under the bed. It was dead. Damn it. I had a sinking feeling that I was going to be late for my rescheduled flight to Argentina.

I eased out of the room, looking for a clock or something to help me navigate the time, or at least my damn phone. I heard the voices outside and made my way out there to find Naseem and Christopher on the patio, playing with airplanes, while the monkey, which I'd learned was named Pedro, sat beside Christopher, snacking on a piece of toast. Something about the sight made my ovaries squeeze, and before I turned away, I heard Christopher's little voice.

"Summer, look, I'm flying a 747."

"That's so cool." I patted his silky-smooth hair. "By any chance, do you know the time or know where my phone is?"

"It's 9:55 a.m.," Naseem said, not even bothering to look up at me.

"No." I covered my face. "I missed my flight."

"I'm guessing it was the margaritas."

The jerk was lucky a kid was standing there, because I would have flipped him off. "I need to call the airport."

"You need a ride to the airport?" Carter and Kendall rounded the corner, each holding a cup of java, and the bittersweet scent was enough to make my mouth water. *Focus. I need to focus.*

"Summer missed her plane," Christopher said in a matter-of-fact tone. "Maybe uncle Nas can take her on his plane. And I can come to be the copilot, again."

"That's a great idea, then you can stay for the reception," Kendall said.

"Oh, I wish I could, but..."

"She has to get to her own wedding." Naseem was only stating facts, but the inflection in his voice could have given us all frostbite.

"Well, let me call the airport. I might have to impose on you guys a little longer if I can't get another flight out."

"I'll keep my fingers crossed that you can stay," Kendall said.

After nursing my hangover with coffee, Tylenol, and a shower, I found my phone in bed. It was vibrating under Catherine's butt and had woken her up. With a clearer head, I checked my call log. My stomach sank when I realized I'd not only missed a few Skype calls from my mom, but also a call from Laith. Guilt washed over me when Laith's name appeared on my screen, and a sort of dread that I didn't want to look at too closely twisted in my gut.

I also had two text messages from my siblings. My sister, Sara, with sincere concern for my well-being, while my brother George's text message left my stomach in knots.

It's a sign from the universe. Come home, he doesn't deserve you.

My brother hadn't tried to interfere with my decision to accept the arranged marriage, but he'd used every chance he could to put doubt in my mind. At first, I believed it was just his unease because I was the baby in the family, but maybe there was something else.

I shook my head. I'd shelve that for later. Right now, I needed to get the fastest plane ticket to Argentina and add miles of distance between Naseem and me.

After being on the phone for close to an hour, I was able to get a new flight, but unfortunately, I was stuck in Rio for two more nights. Two more days and nights under the same roof. I didn't think I'd be able to handle that. So instead of returning my missed calls, I first called around for a hotel room but learned quickly all the hotels were booked for some sort of Romance Book Convention. My only option was to stay here. I would actually be enjoying myself if it wasn't for Naseem sharing the same roof.

My phone buzzed in my hands. And the flashing display read *Mom.* I sighed before answering. My mother's face popped up on the screen.

"Hi, Mom."

"Summer, *bentie*, why haven't you picked up your phone?" My mother didn't even give me a chance to answer her first question—she continued berating me. "I've been worried sick since Laith's mother called to tell me you had plane trouble."

"Mom, calm down. I'm obviously fine since you are looking at my face."

"So where are you and when will you be there?"

I explained about the emergency landing and about bumping into Camille and the family, but I purposely didn't mention Naseem. Less reason for her to worry about my virtue right before my arranged marriage. Not that she knew it was long gone because of Naseem. After I did a lot explaining and lying about my rescheduled flight—because I wasn't going to tell her I missed it because I'd been drinking—it was time for her inspection of me. I had become used to it because of my job and traveling all over the country. This was her way of making sure I was okay even if I was away.

"Let me look at you." She surveyed the screen. "You look sick—are you sick?"

Well, fudge, nothing got by this woman. "No, Mom, I'm just jetlagged."

"Put on some makeup and make sure your hair is styled nice when you fly to Argentina. None of this messy bun hair you like."

I think my eyes rolled into the back of my head. She was the reason I was at the airport in wedges: *"Heels make the legs look skinny."*

"How is Dad?" I interrupted her.

"Your father is making a new mess. He has found another project to do in the house, but he ruined my hardwood floors. Who paints objects in the living room?" I let her go on with her rant about my dad so the heat could be off me.

"Okay, Mom, I have to go. I still need to message Laith my new flight plans."

"Message him? He is your fiancé, you should be speaking on the phone." My throat tightened. "Mom, we talked about this—I have spoken to him, but right now, he's working, and I don't want to bother him," I lied. Again. In this moment, I realized how good I was at lying. But sometimes, I wondered if the lies were for her benefit or for my own.

It took some more work, but I finally got her off my phone.

After I showered and got dressed, I brought my laptop and planner to the patio for some sunshine and work. I knew there was going to be a million emails to get through, and the designer for the new Miami hotel should have sent me updated designs for the dining room for my approval. Sometimes I missed just cooking in the kitchen. Experimenting with flavors, colors, and textures to make the most perfect bite. But right now, I needed to complete my ten-year plan, and going backward in my career goals just wasn't on it. To solidify this, I took out my kikki.K A5 black quilted binder and flipped through my dashboards for my ten-year plan. I couldn't believe that I'd nearly completed everything on the list except getting married.

But I would—by the end of this month, I would have completed everything by my thirtieth birthday.

I should feel relief, but something tugged at my chest. I reached into the right side flap for the vision board I'd created back in senior year with images of the girl that could be me cooking, surrounded by family, and holding a dark-haired baby. I had long removed the picture of Naseem and me at prom from the vision board, but the rest of it had stayed the same. I'd never had the heart to get rid of it. Sometimes, I thought it was a reminder of where I was and what I'd decided to be instead.

The image of the white three-story building I wanted to house my future restaurant gleamed in the sunlight like a jewel. I ran my fingers over the image. Funny thing, it was nearly twelve years later, and that same building was up for sale.

"You still have that?" Naseem's voice behind me left me shook.

"Seriously, you should wear a bell." I attempted to hide the worn paper, but he tugged it out of my hands before I had the chance to put it away.

I rolled my eyes. "Always charming, aren't you?"

"Wasn't there a picture of me on this thing before?" Naseem asked.

"Yes. I burned it."

"I remember this building."

I sat up and tugged my old vision board from his hands.

"Did you ever buy that building?"

"Not that it's any of your business, but I'm the VP of Project Development and Implementation for Lilium, Inc."

"Never heard of them."

"Heard of the Mark Hotel and Resorts? That's just one of the hotels I've helped develop internationally." I knew I sounded like I was bragging, but you know what? Fudge him. He needed to see that I hadn't crumbled after he'd dumped me and I'd actually thrived without him.

"Yeah, I've stayed in the one in Vegas."

"We have one in Rio."

"I'm tempted to call and get a room. I could really use a massage and a night in a hot tub."

"Well, good luck on that. They're completely reserved for a book convention."

"Who does that?"

"I would totally do a book convention. Especially if JK Rowling or JR Ward were there."

"Oh yeah, I remember. You always had a novel in your purse."

"Well, now I have my e-reader. It's like carrying my library in my purse anywhere in the world I go."

"So you don't cook anymore?"

"No, I guess I'm more on the business end of the business instead."

"I remember it used to make you really happy." The sincerity in his voice threw me.

"I squashed a lot of my silly girl dreams and soon realized that my ten-year plan needed to be refined."

"You still have that? A freaking plan?"

His laugh was mocking, and it only served to piss me off. "What's wrong with making plans?"

"Everything. You don't know what's going to happen tomorrow. You can only live for today."

His words hit me like a ton of bricks. He was still the same arrogant asshole who had stood in my face less than twenty-four hours before our trip to say he wasn't going to come with me because he couldn't follow me like a puppy and he needed to live his own life.

This was after he'd planned and mapped out every moment of the trip we were supposed to have taken together. It was the summer before college. The plan was for me to enter the chef's program sponsored by our high school and the community college culinary program because it would allow me to travel, or my strict Chaldean parents wouldn't have agreed to it. While I was working in kitchens, he would do his own exploring. He had a list of adventures he wanted to cross off his own bucket list, but he'd acted like it was all about me.

"You can't live in the moment without structure and plans and goals—you can't grow. Develop."

"That's exactly how I live my life. Every moment is the next adventure."

"Yo, cuz, that's exactly how we do." Rahim came out to the patio, saving me from this ridiculous conversation with Naseem.

Camille came out behind him, looking completely well shagged.

"Are you just now waking up?" I asked her.

"No, we actually were up for a couple hours." She winked at me, and Rahim gave me a very satisfied grin. "Oh, wait, shouldn't you be on a plane?"

"Yes. Thanks to your margaritas, you're stuck sharing your room with me, unless a room frees up at the hotel."

"Absolutely you are staying with me, and you better not argue." She looked between Naseem and me and then smiled. "You never know what fate has in store for you." Camille winked.

"Fate has a surprise for all of you," Carter said, grinning as he and Kendall came out of the house hand in hand.

"I don't like surprises," Camille said.

"You're going to love this one," Kendall assured her.

"Have fun," I said.

"Not a chance, my friend. We are all going. Mom and Dad are enjoying their own adventure, and Cat is staying with the kiddos."

"I have a really bad feeling about this escapade of yours," Camille said.

I had to second Camille's unease. If ever she was apprehensive, I should be just plain terrified because my daredevil friend was never scared.

"No worries, sis, you're going to love it." Carter laughed. "Just one thing–is anyone afraid of heights?"

My stomach sank, and I glanced at Naseem. He beamed and looked at me. "I love heights, but Summer is a little chicken. I think I remember her being petrified from the rides at the state fair."

I glared in the jerk's direction. "I was not," I lied.

"No, hum... Maybe it was another girl who dug her nails into my forearm from fear until I bled."

I rolled my eyes. "Maybe it was Linda Kelly?"

At the sound of her name, his eyes widened. Was that sorrow in his stare? It couldn't be. I was just looking for something that wasn't there. I'd heard he spent the summer sleeping with her after we'd broken up, and the surprised look on his face confirmed it. I wanted to believe so badly that he wouldn't go out with my mortal enemy after dumping me, but how stupid was I, really?

"It wasn't what you think," Naseem said.

"It doesn't matter what I think. Never did," I said.

I busied myself with my planner, not looking at

anything at all. But the tension on the patio was so thick everyone seemed to feel it. I, for one, tasted the bitterness of my words, and my stomach knotted.

"Well, umm, okay. We all leave in like an hour. A car is coming to take us."

"What should we wear?" Camille said.

"Dress like we are hiking. If you have a long-sleeve shirt, wear it, but wear your suits beneath. If we have time, I want you guys to see the most beautiful waterfall," Kendall said.

Swallowing my pride, I had to ask, "Where does the heights thing come into this adventure?"

"Oh, I can't tell you—it's part of the surprise," Carter said.

Naseem's wicked stare found mine and gleamed. "Chicken," he mouthed. I did what any respectable lady would do—I flipped him the bird.

On the way to the room I shared with Camille, I was stopped by Maria Rosa—the cute little lady seemed so eager to tell me something, but I had no clue what she was trying to say.

"She's saying she's seen something about your aura," Carter said.

"Oh, really? I love fortune readings."

"Well, hers aren't always explained as easily as most fortunes."

"What do you mean?"

"You'll see."

Carter directed his attention to Maria Rosa and spoke in Portuguese. He laughed and looked my way, but still kept on in Portuguese.

"What did she say?" I asked when he finally turned to me.

"She said she sees you are having trouble with something blue, but the most important thing you have to remember is to kick your feet."

"What's that supposed to mean?"

"I don't know, but she's usually right on the money."

CHAPTER 5

Hang gliding fucking rocks. The moment Carter mentioned he had a surprise, I knew we were coming here. It was his favorite sport, and both he and I had been trained to do this since college. Rahim was too—it was one of the first lessons I had him take when he started working for me.

Our group took the hour-and-a-half required exercise, and I knew how this was going to play out—with me paired with Summer. Carter was flying with his wife, Rahim had spent the better part of last night and this morning banging Camille, so that just left me and Summer. Yeah, like I said, this shit was going to be interesting.

I mean, the truth is, I wasn't disappointed. From the moment I'd pulled her near drowning body out of the water and pressed it flush against mine, I'd wanted to feel her against me again. I wanted to taste her, see her squirm beneath my tongue. I desired to watch that smart-ass mouth of hers yield to me. But she was engaged, to none other than that piece of shit, Laith.

I still couldn't get over it. Why in the world was she marrying him? And I was having a hard time believing the romantic long-distance-relationship bullshit that she was trying to spew to us.

"And Summer, you're with Naseem."

"What? No. What about the instructors?" Summer took a step back away from me.

"I'm an instructor. All three of us are," I said.

"Oh, this is going to be more fun than I thought." Camille placed her arms around Rahim.

"Unless you're scared," I goaded Summer.

"No, I'm not scared." She lifted her chin and stared straight into my eyes. Pure hatred glared back at me.

"Yes, this is going to be a blast," I mocked. I suited up first before I went over to help her. She only relented because she was completely overwhelmed by this entire process.

After making sure she was completely buckled—I had to maneuver around her fanny pack since the girl was always prepared—I fastened myself before I led us to the starting point with everyone else.

"Are you guys ready?" Carter called out. There were some cheers from the rest of us, but not my partner. I knew she was quaking in her Nikes.

"Listen, it's going to be really fun."

"Are you sure you know what you're doing?"

"Yes, I've been flying these for years. There was a time that Carter and I spent a whole summer doing this."

Her shoulders eased. She closed her eyes for five heartbeats and took a long breath, like the ones they do in yoga. Not that I've ever taken a class. But I was sure with her fit form she was a regular in yoga class.

"Okay, stand behind me and hold on."

Her arms wrapped around my waist.

"Tighter," I said.

Her curves stretched over my back, and I suppressed a groan. I was already hard, because I was about to fly having her pressed against me. Well, I could just come in my pants.

Then, we were moving and then dropping. The moment we dropped, she yelped, and her legs wrapped around my waist.

"Holy fuck... We're going to die," she screamed.

"Hold on, we're going to..." Before I could even finish my sentence, we started floating up and gliding on air.

"Oh my God." Her warm breath right below my earlobe sent a tremble through my body. "I can't look." Her head pushed into my back.

"Summer, you have to open your eyes."

"No. I can't look." Her hands tightened on my shirt.

"Sweet pea, you can't miss this."

"What is it?"

"You'll have to open your eyes to see."

"You're just lying to make me look." She pressed her face between my shoulder blades, the sweet scent of her shampoo washing over me.

"I'm not, and you're going to regret missing it."

I angled us toward the gorgeous Christ the Redeemer statue of Jesus.

"Oh, it's so beautiful, even from here." Her voice whispered in my ear.

"Yeah, it is." My heart ached. Being with her, this way, so close, reminded me of the trip we should have taken together—if fate wasn't so cruel.

"I can't stop looking at it."

"Want to take a closer look?"

"Yes." The ache in my heart warmed at the excitement in her voice. At least destiny had given us one last do-over before I lost her to another man forever.

~

IF SOMEONE WOULD HAVE TOLD ME LAST WEEK THAT I'd be flying around Rio de Janeiro on the back of Naseem Kakos, I'd have asked if they ate a batch of funny brownies, because never in a million years would I have imagined seeing him, much least perching on his back and hang gliding. But I was mesmerized and nearly forgot my fears—not completely, but almost.

I let him lead me around the city, seeing one sight after the next, and in my perusal view, noticed that we'd somehow lost the rest. It was just him and me in this big bright blue sky over a really large body of water.

"We lost the others."

"It's okay, I know where we are." He sounded confident, but it didn't ease the creeping fear in my chest. We had just circled near the magnificent Sugarloaf when the wind picked up, and we seemed to be flying in a different direction than I thought Naseem had intended.

"Shouldn't we be going left?" I tightened my hold around him. Seriously, if he were a girl, I'd be cupping his breasts, that's how intimate this whole ride seemed.

"Yes."

The sail dipped lower, a little too fast for my shattered nerves. My pulse quickened and there was this new whirling sound in my ears.

"Fuck."

"What?" I glued my body tighter to his. My fear made me want to climb into his skin for safety.

"There's a hole in the sail and we are going to have to land sooner than expected."

I looked up. He was right. I could see the hole in the fabric, and that whirling sound I was hearing had come from it. I looked down, and my heart sank. Water surrounded us.

"Are we going to make it to land?"

"Maybe. If we don't descend any faster, we might."

His tone was something I'd never heard. Serious, confident, but grave. He was forever playful or arrogant, but at this moment, he was in charge and level-headed, and if it wasn't for the fact that my life was flashing before my eyes, I'd be swooning all over him.

We were moving faster now. Almost like a magical string was pulling us through the air at a rapid speed. But we were also moving away from the water and closer to land.

"Do you think we can avoid the water?"

"I'm trying."

"Oh my God. Oh my God."

"Summer."

"We are just going to crash, right into the ocean. There are sharks in the ocean. Naseem. Oh my God, Naseem. I can't do this."

"Sweet pea." He used the nickname he used to use to call me back in high school again. And it worked just as it had with my last tantrum. I froze.

"We got this."

My meltdown had apparently lasted a while, or we were moving even faster, because now the water was only a few yards away. But luckily, Naseem had somehow managed to get us just a few swimming feet of distance to the shore. I closed my eyes tight. I couldn't look as we plummeted closer to the blue body of water filled with sharks and creepy crawly things. So I wasn't prepared when the cold, salty water swallowed me. I reached to grip Naseem tighter, but his strong body wasn't beneath my own. My heart pounded. I kicked my feet as hard as I could. But swimming in Nikes was hard. The saltwater burning my eyes, I finally made it to the surface. Alone.

"Naseem." My heart sank, along with my body that struggled to stay afloat. "Oh, my God, Naseem." Where did he go? We'd been fucking attached. How in the world had we separated?

Something grabbed me from behind and I screamed bloody murder. A shark was going to eat me, and I was going to die an old maid. I kicked my feet harder, and Carter's voice came to mind: "*She said kick your feet.*"

Oh shit, Maria Rosa had warned me to kick my feet.

CHAPTER 6

It was a matter of moments. I was able to undo our harnesses just as we were about to drop into the water. I knew that damn sail was going to cover us, and I didn't want the extra weight to drag us down. After kicking off the sail, I spotted Summer easily in the crystal-clear ocean. But she was being dragged down by the waves and not able to keep her head afloat.

I swam with everything I had and reached her just as she started to go under again. We were actually only a few yards from the shore, but it looked like this part of the ocean was still pretty deep since we couldn't stand. I dove under and, taking hold of her, pressed her body against mine and kicked us to the surface.

She yelped and wiggled in my arms. "Hey, it's me. I got you."

"Naseem?"

"Yes, sweet pea, I got you." She stopped fighting me, but she was trembling in my arms.

"You think you can swim?"

"Yes..."

"Okay, on three. One. Two. Three."

I let her go first, so I could keep an eye on her. I could tell she was struggling, but she wasn't a quitter. So we swam. For a moment, it felt like we were reenacting the movie *Open Water*. I couldn't see anyone, no boats or people on the beach. It was strange. I'd noticed from the sky, when we'd started to drop, that there wasn't anyone in sight.

We finally made it to shore. Soaked, gasping, and completely exhausted, we lay side by side on the sand for a moment to catch our breath.

"Are you okay?" I was finally able to lift my head, and the first thing I did was check to make sure she wasn't injured. After examining all her limbs for any open wounds, I searched her face. Her eyes were closed, chest heaving, and her hair was a tangled mess around her face—but she was still the most beautiful girl I'd ever laid eyes on. Her perfect, pouty lips parted while she panted to catch her breath, and she had the sexiest beauty mark just left of her adorable little nose that I ached to kiss just once.

In those few moments when I'd watched her struggle in the water, I'd realized I was still fucking in love with this woman. I brushed the wet hair from her eyes and caressed her cheek, my finger adorning the spot I'd desperately wanted to trace with my lips.

She leaned her face into my hand, and her lips trembled before her eyes shot open and she pushed my hand away. She struggled but stood anyway.

"So, where are we?"

I took off my Nikes and socks because I hated wet feet. "I don't know."

"I don't see anyone." She paced the beach. "It's like

we just landed in front of the freaking jungle or something."

I stood and took off my joggers.

"What are you doing?" She leaped back, but her eyes weren't on my face.

"I'm wearing my swimming trunks, relax."

"Oh...good."

"Are you wearing your suit underneath?"

"Yes."

"My eyes are up here." I smirked.

She rolled her eyes. "Don't flatter yourself." But her cheeks flushed.

"Take off your clothes so that they dry."

She looked uneasy for a moment, then, in a really seductive way, she unzipped her black hoodie and exposed the little hot pink triangles that barely covered her nipples. The jacket slipped off her shoulders and down her arms. My breath caught. My dick was totally hard. She bent to lay her jacket in the sand next to mine and her tits swayed and bounced in the delicious way they do when they are a perfect DD.

"Kakos, my eyes are up here." She laughed. I adjusted my hard-on and pretended to busy myself trying to look around for anything that would tell me where we were.

"That behind us is Tijuca Forest," I said.

"You've been here?" she asked.

"Yes. A long time ago, I traveled through with some buddies."

"So you know how to get us to civilization?"

"Well, we had a tour guide, but I think so."

When I turned back around, she was only wearing her bikini. Her yoga pants, hoodie, and pink Nikes were drying next to my clothes. I moved my gaze to her bent-over body while she was brushing her hair off her face. All her body parts seemed to sway with every stroke of the brush.

Was it even possible for my dick to get harder? "Where did you get that brush?"

"My fanny pack."

"What else do you have in there?"

"What are you looking for?"

"A phone? Maybe something to eat, or...never mind, it would be ruined because of the water."

"No, my bag is waterproof, and I have like twelve protein bars in there. And yes, my phone."

She hurried over to the bag and pulled out her phone. "Damn it, no service."

"What about you?

"Nope, I left it in the car at the gliding site."

She circled the beach with her phone pointed to the sky. "It's no use, I'm not getting anything. But here, take a protein bar."

"Not that I'm complaining, because right now, I'm extremely grateful, but twelve?"

"Yes, there were six of us coming out, so I brought two for each."

"The Chaldean woman who must feed everyone."

"Yeah, I guess that part is embedded in my DNA."

She handed me a protein bar and took one herself, and we sat in the sun, eating. The heat on my back, the roar of waves, the birds chirping, her beside me. A peace washed over me, and the world finally felt right for the first time in a very long time.

"I missed us." I didn't mean to say the words, but my mouth had its own mind, apparently.

"You don't get to say that to me."

"I'm sorry. There so much you don't know."

"Don't."

"Sweet pea." I reached for her, but she waved me away.

"Never call me that again. You lost your chance when you accused me of trying to make you my puppy. You lost that chance when I begged you to not end things, but you told me I was holding you back. You lost that chance when you broke my fucking heart."

She stormed away. Sand kicked in her wake and covered me. I watched her walking toward the other side of the shore and I let her go. She needed to cool down, but I kept a close eye on her because the last thing we needed was for us to separate while we were essentially lost.

But it was time to come clean. Her words gutted me. She seemed so together now, I almost forgot the tears in her big brown eyes. The pain of that dreaded year of my life hit me like a ton of bricks.

It was the day after graduation and everyone that was going to Spain had to report to the high school. Since I wasn't part of the actual program, I didn't have to attend the meeting, but it was my last opportunity to tell Summer I wasn't going on the trip and convince her to go without me. My hands shook. Every fiber of my being dreaded lying to Summer, but there was no other way.

I'd rehearsed my speech a million times, but all words escaped me when I found her sitting on the lawn cross-legged, her dark waves floating down her back and her face covered with a book firmly in hand. She always took my breath away.

She sensed me watching her, and her eyes sparkled when our gazes met.

"Hey."

I sat beside her but still, the words didn't come. I debated telling her the truth, but honestly, she would cancel her trip too. And I didn't want to take this opportunity away from her. When else was she going to be able to travel through Europe and work in kitchens, try exotic food, just experience life? I couldn't do that to her. So I had no choice but to break her heart and mine.

"Hey, listen, I have to tell you something."

"What's up?"

"I... I'm not coming to Spain." I spewed the words.

"What? Why?" The shock in her face almost made me come clean, but I restrained the urge.

"Look, cooking is your thing, not mine. And, I'm not going to follow you around like a puppy and not live my life." The lie burned like acid on my tongue.

"I thought you wanted to go..." The hurt in her voice nearly broke me, but I held it together for her sake, and for my own.

"You assumed, and I just went along with your plans. But not anymore."

"Okay, that's okay. If you don't want to go, we don't have to."

"Always with the 'we.' I'm my own person, and you're just holding me back."

She recoiled like I'd slapped her. Tears pooled in her eyes and streamed down her face. My hands trembled to wipe them away, to hold her close to me, to tell her the truth. Because honestly, I needed her, her comfort, her arms, her body, her laugh. I needed every fucking part of her. And right now, watching her crumble, I was sick.

"You want to break up?"

Her words were whispered but echoed to the very depths of my soul. No. I didn't want to break up. *No, I don't want you to go without me to Spain. No, I don't think I can do all of this without you. No.*

"Yes. We've been together for like all of high school. It's time for us to see other people."

The acid burned and seethed through my stomach, and I estimated only a few moments before I lost my lunch.

"Please don't do this..."

"I got to go." Hot coals moved up my chest, and my eyes burned with unshed tears.

I'd shot to my feet and run to the parking lot but only made it halfway before I'd fallen to my knees on hard gravel and emptied the contents of my stomach.

I'M SO STUPID. HOW IN THE WORLD COULD I LET Naseem get under my skin like that? How could I show him how he still affected me? How I was broken on the inside because of what he did to me all those years ago? After he'd run off and left me calling after him, I'd just crumbled on the lawn of the school, completely lost and devastated.

It was Camille who'd found me. That was how we'd become friends. She'd stayed to talk to Miss Reyna after the meeting because she was coming along on our trip as a mentor since she'd already done the Inspiring Chef program a couple years before.

She'd been there for me. She was the shoulder I cried on, the source of my strength while I attempted to heal from the biggest heartbreak of my life. The problem was, I couldn't wrap my head around the things he'd said to me. Not after all we'd shared. Not after I'd loved him basically my whole adolescent life. He broke me in ways that I never healed from, and that was the reason I'd decided to agree to an arranged marriage. I didn't want to open my heart to anyone else. I'm embarrassed to say that even my sexual encounters had been commitment-free.

"Summer, can we talk?"

I hated that his voice still made my insides warm and my heart race. I hated that. I wanted to hate him, and I just couldn't find it in my heart to dislike him, no matter how much I really wanted to.

"There's nothing to say."

"I think there's a few things that I should confess."

"We need to find our way off this beach and back to civilization. We do not have time for unneeded conversations."

"My dad had three months to live."

It was like someone threw a bucket of ice water in my face. "What?"

"The day before we were supposed to leave for Spain, we learned that my dad had stage four lung cancer. We were completely broken and shattered as a family. I had to stay behind. I couldn't go with you, despite how much I wanted to run away with you that day and not face my father's mortality. "

"I'm sorry. Your dad was a really nice man."

He nodded. As the shock of what he'd just said wore off and his words started to sink in, I turned to face him. "So wait, what about the things you said to me?"

"I didn't mean any of those things. Not one word."

"So you fought with me, made me hate you, and shattered the foundation of my mental state because you couldn't man up and tell me the truth?" The shock and sympathy I was feeling had completely worn off, and white hot anger washed over me.

"Would you have gone to Spain if I'd told you the truth?"

"No, I would have stayed with you."

"That's exactly why I did what I did."

It was like another ice-cold bucket doused me. And the sobering realization of what he'd done completely sank in.

"You broke things off in that despicable way because it was the only way to completely push me away. You knew those hateful words would make it so I'd never want to see you again."

When I looked over at him, he was facing the ocean, but the sun shined on his features and illuminated the tears that rimmed his dark eyes. I caressed his cheek and wiped a single tear that escaped his lid.

He leaned into my hand, and his eyes closed. "It was the hardest thing I have ever done, next to mourning both my parents in a matter of months of each other."

"Your Mom too? Oh my God, how?"

"Heart attack. I'm pretty sure she died of a broken heart." He raised the gold cross hanging from the chain around his neck and brought it to his lips. It was the first time I noticed there was a diamond band beside the chain.

"This is theirs." His fingers twisted. "My father's cross, and my mother's wedding band." I haven't taken it off since. It helps me feel like they're still with me."

I clasped his free hand. "I didn't know any of this. I'm so sorry."

"I'm surprised. I figured the Chaldean community is small enough that you would have heard."

"I would have come to the funerals if I'd known."

"After everything I said to you that day, I wouldn't have deserved it."

"I wouldn't have come for you. You know I really loved Nash. It was your brother that I secretly pined after."

He laughed, and the tension in his face lifted. "You and he used to remind me of this often."

His warm hand covered mine, and my body completely responded.

"Seriously, though," he said, "I am sorry for everything I said that day. I wasn't thinking right. I couldn't see past my current situation, but I didn't mean any of it. I was so in love with you. I need you to know that."

"Well, I appreciate you telling me. Honestly, it's a lot to process. I don't know how I'm supposed to feel or how and where we are supposed to go from here."

"I mean, we could kiss and make up."

I laughed. "Keep dreaming." Though every inch of my body really wanted his mouth on mine. "Come on, we better get a move on through the forest. I don't think a rescue team is coming."

Our clothes were still a little too damp to wear, so we gathered our things and put on our Nikes for the long journey through the forest—a foreign, remote forest filled with unknown creatures. Ugh, probably bugs, and snakes.

"Oh God, are there lions or tigers or bears in this forest?"

"Oh yeah, and they really like the color hot pink."

I looked down at my bikini. "You're joking, right?"

"Am I?" He winked.

CHAPTER 7

Summer's ass in that hot pink bikini bottom just might be the death of me. I was torn between falling back and watching the perfect apple-shaped cheeks bounce in front of me or moving in front of her to get sex off my mind. I decided to speed up my pace so that we walked at the same speed and I could just get a quick glance every now and then—because, well, I'm a horn dog.

"How are your siblings?" Since we hadn't talked in nearly an hour, she flinched at my words.

"They hate you." A small, sly smile tugged at her lips while she kept her eyes peeled on our never-ending trail.

"Hate me, huh? You know, George came to my father's funeral."

"My brother? Really? He didn't tell me anything, but I'm assuming he came for Nash."

She was right, even though George did pay his condolences to me. I knew he not-so-secretly believed I'd failed his baby sister, broken the promise I'd made to him, and I couldn't blame the guy. Summer truly didn't deserve what I'd done all those years ago. God, I was such an asshole.

"George is married to Renee. You remember her? She was in our year."

"Of course I remember. She was always at your house whenever I called you."

Summer's laugh was like sunshine on a cloudy day and filled cold places in my soul that had been cold so long, I'd forgotten how warmth could feel.

"Yeah, she crushed on him for years and finally succeeded in getting him to see her as more than his baby sister's friend."

"That's why she wouldn't date the guys that seemed to be lined up for her." I remembered Renee. She was gorgeous, and all my friends had tried to go out with her, but she hadn't given any of them the time of day.

"Yeah, everyone thought she was stuck-up, but she was just totally crushing on George, and because of her persistence, I have the cutest niece and nephews."

"Wow, George is a dad?"

"Yup, can you imagine? He's becoming a version of my dad. It's the funniest thing."

Something about hearing those words shook me. Maybe because I wouldn't ever become a dad myself. A sense of loss I didn't quite understand plagued me.

"Sara was engaged when we...that summer before Spain." She stuttered over her words, but I heard the "when you dumped me" behind her mumbling. "And has basically four teenagers at home."

"Your parents are probably on cloud nine with all those grandchildren."

"You should see my dad. He never once played soccer

with us as kids, but with the grandkids, he's like Cristiano Ronaldo."

"I can't even picture it."

"Hang on." She reached into her fanny pack and pulled out her phone. "Ugh, still no service, but look at these pictures I took the morning before I left for the airport."

She'd stopped in the middle of the trail and started scrolling through her pictures, but all I could see was the bright light that shone through while she spoke about her family. My heart ached.

"Here, look at him."

"Is your dad actually wearing a Cristiano jersey?" I laughed.

"Yes, and he has matching ones for my nephews." She scrolled through the images and stopped at a picture of Mr. Seba, two teenage boys, and one little one that could maybe be Christopher's age, held by George.

"Where did George's hair go?"

"Well, he started going bald in the front, so he just shaved it off. He didn't want to rock my dad's look so soon." She laughed. "We tease him about it all the time."

I stared down at the image of three generations of men and my chest tightened. I'd pushed down so many emotions for so long, and it was like seeing Summer had flooded the gates wide open.

Her fingers moved around the scene of little square images when one caught my attention. "Who is that?" Anger fueled inside my gut.

"That's, umm, Laith."

"The fiancé." I snatched the phone from her fingertips before she could even react.

"Give it back." Her little fist jabbed into my torso, but I didn't feel a thing but light caresses on my skin.

"If you want to feel me up, that's not the right way. Has it been so long you've forgotten?"

I turned my back and zoomed in on the image. "He still looks like an *ufftie* to me."

"You don't have to insult him." This time, her jab was a little more aggressive, and I relented and handed her the phone.

"I just call 'em like I see 'em."

"You think I'm marrying a loser."

"No, its meaning is much more than just simply a loser."

"You always assumed you understood the Arabic language better than me, so please enlighten me."

"An *ufftie* is a man who doesn't have magnetism. No real strength to his personality, a lack of character, a simpleton... Should I go on?"

"You're impossible." A sharp pain nudged my side and caught me off guard. "That's for being a total jerk."

"Your love pats are really turning me on."

She rolled her eyes. "Are you sure you know where we are? Because I can't see any civilization anywhere."

"Yeah, about that, I'm pretty sure this is Tijuca Forest, but I think we might have landed on the opposite end of the forest."

"What does that mean?" She waved her hands in the air, swatting away a bug that seemed to be enamored with her.

"I'm not sure which way to the camping sites."

"Oh, God, we're going to be stuck here all night." The look of horror on her face might have been adorable had I not been freaking out about the same thing.

"I don't know, but let's keep going and make the best use of the light hours."

She turned away with a huff, flapping her arms around her in what looked like an attempt to get a signal on her phone. "'Let's go hang gliding,' they said. 'It will be fun,' they said. Of all the senseless, rash, and reckless ideas."

I muffled a chuckle and followed that sexy, angry ass down the trail to hell-knew-where. "At least the view is beautiful."

Her gorgeous mane of wild hair flipped over her sun-kissed shoulder, and her piercing stare bored into my own. I made no attempt to hide my lust while my gaze traveled down to her ass and back to her face. Though she hid it well with her prissy glare, she enjoyed my gaze on her body. She bit down on her lower lip, and her cheeks flushed with the cutest shade of pink.

"You can kiss the beautiful view." With that, she stormed off into the lush green trees, and I had to quicken my steps to keep up with her.

"Anytime, sweetheart, anytime."

"You're just impossible." She spoke without turning to look at me, but I watched as her hips had a little more bounce with every word I spoke.

"That's not a no."

Her laugh invoked one of my own. "It's not a yes."

"Honestly, if you were stuck on a deserted island, I would totally be one of your top three picks."

"Considering we are in a deserted forest, I'm really *not* happy that it's you."

"Bet you're happier it's me than Laith."

Her step faltered, but this time, she didn't reply, and I had a feeling I'd just hit the nail on the head.

Well, fudge. He was right, and I hated to acknowledge it. I'd had more fun almost dying and getting lost in a strange forest with Naseem than I wanted to admit. For one thing, watching all the hard muscle, naked man chest, and rock-hard forearms for the past hour was torture for any healthy man-loving libido, but having touched them and once been wrapped around them was making my body respond in ways that I'd thought had forgotten to know how to work. My breasts ached, my stomach hummed with desire, and between my legs purred every time his mischievous smile turned my way.

"Do you have music saved on your phone?" His delicious smoky voice just behind me added to the hunger waging war inside me.

"Yeah, I have tons." My voice sounded strange to my own ears. I slowed down my pace and pulled out my phone. "What do you want to listen to?"

"Freestyle?"

"No." At the memory of the previous night's freestyle session and all the buried feelings those songs ignited, I answered a little too quickly. "I'll just put it on shuffle. There's like two thousand songs on here from the eighties to late two-thousands, before Apple music and Spotify started subscriptions."

"So just the old stuff. I'm good with that. I like it better than new music anyway."

I pressed play, and Britney Spears's "Baby One More Time" blared my little speaker.

"Yes, Britney. I feel like we're still in high school." He did some move that was supposed to be cool, and it might have been back in the day, but at the moment, he looked like a complete dork.

I shook my head and continued the trail to God-knew-where, his last statement still ringing in my ears. It did feel like we were back in high school. Just me and him, half naked and listening to music. Granted, back then, we couldn't keep our hands off each other. It was a good thing I had more restraint now than I'd had as a teenager.

"Do you remember this song?" Naseem's voice was like a soft kiss on my aching skin.

I'd been so lost in my thoughts I hadn't realized the track had changed to "My Love" by Justin Timberlake, and my heart fluttered. He surely couldn't remember that was the song that had been playing in the background when we'd had our first kiss.

"Yeah, I remember. I love Justin's music."

"Man, I was so nervous that day. I couldn't believe that Nash and George left us alone. Together. I knew I'd probably never get a chance like that again."

"What are you talking about?" I played coy, but he didn't know that song was a reminder to me of both the happiest and saddest times.

"You don't remember the song that was playing when we had our first kiss?"

"I...I remember." I stopped walking and turned to face him, and fire burned back at me from beneath his heated stare. "I didn't think you would remember."

"I remember every moment with you." He stepped closer to me. "I remember how you tasted of cherry lip gloss and cinnamon gum." He took another step closer. "You used to wear that stuff from Victoria's Secret that smelled like strawberry and cream. I remember how just before I'd kiss you, you'd dart your gaze away because you would get self-conscious."

He was standing before me, his naked chest nearly pressing against my aching breasts, his warm breath kissing my face. My body leaned in farther, closing the space between us, my chest heaving like I'd been running.

"You remember all of that," I whispered.

"I remember so much more."

My mind and my body were in full combat. My mind told me I had to step back, that I couldn't go down this road, but my body was humming in sexual need and frustration. But then his gaze traveled to somewhere above my face.

"Summer, don't move. There's something on you."

CHAPTER 8

"Oh my God, oh my God, what's on me?" Summer was bouncing around, her tits shaking, her wild hair flying around her face, and her arms waving about like she was fighting an invisible enemy. "Get it off of me, get it off."

I steadied her by taking her arms. "Hang on, let me see."

"Don't move." I watched the lizard holding on to her hair for dear life.

"Oh my God, what is it? What is it?"

"It's no big deal, but I need my hands, so stop moving around." I tried to speak in a calming voice, but to be honest, I was super wigged out myself. I hadn't been the type of boy who liked to play with creatures. I had been a hardcore PlayStation gamer, and since my parents worked, there wasn't anyone to make me go outside and play. So needless to say, my dick decided it wasn't horny anymore.

"Okay, please hurry." Her voice trembled, and, oh

God, she was crying. I reached up and took it off her head and placed it on the grass.

She recoiled. "That thing was on me." She shook out her hair like she'd been part of a metal band. "I need a shower. I'm thirsty and hungry. How much longer?"

"I don't know."

"We are never getting out of here. Are we actually going to stay here in the dark?" She covered her face with her hands.

I pulled her to me, wrapping my arms around her. "Hey, hey, it's okay. I'll get us out of here, I promise." Man, she felt amazing in my arms, her curves melted into me, her perfect breasts pressed against my chest, my arms wrapped around the smooth skin of her tanned waist. She surprised me by wrapping her own arms around my waist, and she pulled us flesh against flesh. Of course, my dick took that exact moment to come back to attention and kick against her belly.

Her head lifted, and our eyes met. So many questions and insecurities seemed to stare back at me. I brushed the strands of wild hair from her face and then cupped her cheek. She stared at me in bewilderment.

"You are so beautiful." I leaned and waited with my mouth just over hers. She closed her eyes and parted her lips.

I groaned and closed the space between us, softly kissing and exploring her. She whimpered and let me taste her sweet, minty flavor. Her fingers teased over the strained muscles in my back and stomach, then wrapped around my neck, leaving tremors in her wake. She pulled me closer and gave me further access to her. I caressed her smooth neck and down the silky soft skin of her back. My palm cupped her ass, and she let out a delicious little sigh.

I was whirling with a shitload of lust and desire. But mostly, I felt so much love for this woman, my heart exploded with it. My head was dizzy with it.

I traveled a path down her neck and kissed that special place behind her ear that I knew she loved.

"Naseem."

Fuck, I missed the way she moaned my name.

It made me feel all caveman and powerful. I cupped her ass, lifted her off the ground, and pressed her back against a tree. Then I realized that would probably hurt her, so I turned us and leaned my back against the tree instead.

"Fuck, give me that mouth." She cupped my face and kissed me, hard and passionate, and a little messy. I felt her heat through her bikini bottoms and against my growing, needy cock in my shorts.

Things were escalating really hot and fast, and I savored every second of it.

She broke the kiss and stared down at me with lust-filled eyes. Her lips swollen from my mouth on hers, her chest heaving, she started to rock against my dick.

"We can't do this," she panted.

"Can't what?" I squeezed her ass cheeks and worked her wet and warm bottom over my rock-hard cock through my shorts. I forgot how good clothes burning could be.

She moaned. "This. Us. It's not right." She didn't stop moving against me, though. Instead, she threw her head back and bit down on her lip.

"This doesn't feel right?" I teased her neck and moved toward the mouthwatering swells of her breasts. "I remember making you come with my mouth here." I nuzzled her breasts with my face.

"Show me."

I bit the corner of her bikini top and tugged with my teeth.

She slid the little hot pink triangle to the side and teased me with beautiful swollen nipples. Then she ran her fingers over the swell like they ached. Fuck.

"You're fucking perfection."

She took my face in her hands and kissed the living daylights out of me while we clothes burned. Her hands on my hair, me gripping her ass, she tossed her head back and gave me access to her tits. I feasted. Tasted, licked, sucked. Nipped. The sweet, salty taste of her drove me wild with need. Her moans and sexy sounds added fuel to my passion. My body burned to have her on her knees and taking all of me. Then, she screamed.

At first, I thought I'd made her orgasm, but then I realized her shout was in horror. "What is it?"

"A snake. Up there." She pointed toward the tree we were, of course, leaning on. I quickly moved us away.

"That's an ugly one."

"It's okay. Maybe we should've found a better spot."

I set her down and checked her face, but she was averting her eyes. "Look at me, Summer. You alright?"

"Yeah, it's just that must have been a sign that we shouldn't have done that."

"Why? We both were really enjoying it."

"Because, technically, I'm engaged."

Fury raged through me. Was she for real? She had literally just climbed me like a fucking tree, and now she remembered she was technically engaged?"

"Right, to Laith. When was the last time you saw him?"

"A couple weeks ago."

"No, I mean in person."

"That doesn't matter. It's none of your business."

"I have every right to ask after what just happened between us." Heat boiled under my skin. "He went to Spain with you and Camille, right? Was he your rebound?"

"You have no right to ask me that, because I'm sure you fucked plenty of women that summer, including Linda Kelly. Because she actually made sure I heard all about it as soon as I got home that summer."

"So you did fuck him in Spain."

"I didn't say that." She picked up her things and shook them off with a force that would probably scare the snake and stalked off through the path.

"I'm hearing things, or do you hear running water?" She stopped in her tracks.

"I remember this. Just up there is the Tijuca waterfall."

"Is it fresh water?"

"Yeah." I was still angry, my dick was still painfully hard, and I hated that, despite her engagement to that *efftie*, I still wanted her in any way I could get her.

We followed the sound of water and then we reached the waterfalls. A tremendous pool and a beautiful set of stairs led up to the top of the waterfall. We kicked off our shoes and climbed up to the stream. Which was good timing, because the sun was setting and it looked like we would have to camp out here for the night.

Fuck, water had never tasted so luscious in my life. After washing my face and hands, I really needed to find a way to relieve this hard-on because I wasn't going to be able to do shit until I did.

"Hey, it's getting dark. By any chance do you have matches in that bag of yours?"

"No. But I have a lighter."

"Seriously?"

"Yeah, don't judge me, but sometimes I smoke when I drink."

"I didn't see you smoking and you drank a lot."

"Camille and I sneaked a smoke when no one was watching."

"That's actually good. We'll probably have to camp out for the night right here."

She licked her lips and averted her eyes. "Umm, okay, I'll probably wash up. Thank God I put a clean bikini in my bag."

"You packed an extra?"

"Yeah, you know, I'm a planner. I figured if we went to that beach place Kendall wanted to go to, I would have to travel back in a wet suit. I hate wet suits."

"You amaze me."

She shrugged. "Who would have thought my organizational skills would make me perfect for *Survivor*?"

"I'll wash up too, but I'll probably just go commando since I'm not as prepared as you are."

Her eyes traveled down my body, and I let her get a good, long look at my hard dick that was crying for attention inside my shorts before making my way down the stairs and jumping into the pool. It was colder than I expected, but after being in the hot sun all day, it felt good on my skin.

I floated on my back and let the water cover me. My cock ached, and I finally caressed the motherfucker through my shorts. I glanced in Summer's direction, and she licked her lips and touched her breasts. But I don't even think she was aware she was doing it. She was just as aroused as I was. Fuck her pussy-ass fiancé. My gut told me something was really off with that situation. I was actually able to stand in part of the pool, and I worked my shorts off my hips and swam butt-ass naked toward where she was perched, watching me.

"Can you hold on to these for me?" I tossed her my shorts, and she caught them without a word, but the lust and desire radiated from her eyes.

I let her get a good look at my ass and cock before I swam a few feet away.

Her eyes were still trained on me, though she pretended to busy herself. She'd jumped into the pool but stayed in the shallow end. She stood below the last step of the waterfall and let water run down her hair and breasts. The little squares weren't strong enough to hold the weight of her DDs in the vast pressure of the waterfall, and her top came off. But she didn't seem to mind or care that I could see her. Instead, she seemed to relish the feel of the water on her skin, and she caressed her body in the way I longed to.

I leaned back against the rocks and watched her. Fuck, she was so freaking beautiful and sexy. Her hands moved over each breast, slowly and seductively. Her eyes bored into my own, and she let her fingers roam down her stomach to the edge of her pink bottoms.

I swam closer to her and joined her beneath the waterfall. I let the cool, clear water wash over my chest and body while my eyes stayed on her.

"Do you remember the first time we masturbated together?"

"Yes." Her lips quivered.

"Do you remember why we did?" My hands moved down my stomach and made one smooth pass over my dick. Her fingers tightened on one beautiful tit and caressed while watching me.

"Because masturbating isn't sex."

I gripped my cock, and I worked myself up and down my shaft under the water. Our eyes met, and one of her delicate hands circled her nipple and squeezed while the other roamed down her stomach.

Her gaze burned with a challenge while she slid her fingers inside her bottoms, and a little moan escaped her lips. I groaned.

She touched herself while I watched. I wanted it to be me, my hands on her breasts and my fingers inside her delicious, wet pussy. My hand worked harder over my shaft. She moaned again and pressed her back against the stone wall behind us, but her eyes were on all of me.

"I want to be touching you, Summer. I want to fuck you with my hands."

"Yes."

"You want me inside you Summer?" I moved closer to her, my lips just over her ear. "Are you imagining my hands inside that sweet pussy, my mouth on your clit?"

"Yes."

"Show me that wet pussy, let me taste it."

She moved back from the waterfall and perched on a rock. Her hands teased beneath the little pink bottoms.

"Show me," I ordered.

She spread her legs and pushed the little fabric to expose her pussy. "Like this?" Her words trembled on her lips.

"Baby, I need to see all of you."

She caressed herself over the fabric before unlacing the strings on her hips that knotted the bikini bottoms together. The fabric gave, and she was completely bare to me.

"Fuck, Summer." I moved my hands over my dick. "Now touch yourself, I want to see your fingers moving in and out of that beautiful wet pussy."

Her eyes locked with mine, and I moved closer. I wanted to fall between her legs and feast on her. I wanted her hands in my hair, pressing my face against her clit.

"I want to taste you. Do you still taste how I remember?" I was standing over her, my cock hard and almost nearing its release. "Will you let me taste you?"

"Naseem."

A beautiful orgasm rocked her, and the sight of her unraveling triggered my own release. I turned away so that I wouldn't orgasm on her, but her voice surprised me.

"I want to see you."

We locked stares. Her beautiful, naughty lips parted while she continued to draw out her release. My body trembled from the need to let go.

"Come for me, Naseem." Her words rocked through me, and I came with her name on my lips.

Afterward, the magic ended. She stood up from her perch and didn't even look my way. Like it never happened, like it didn't mean shit to her. Like *I* still didn't mean shit to her. Just here for her amusement. One minute, she was actually riding my dick, and the next, she was pushing me away. The following moment, she was acting out a dirty scene from one of her romance novels.

But I don't know what I was expecting—maybe her acknowledgment of our unresolved feelings, or maybe just the sexual tension, but either way, I wanted her to admit to something, anything.

No, no. What the hell did I just do? Holy fritter, did I just masturbate in front of my ex-boyfriend in a forest after I'd explicitly told him it was a bad idea to get sexual since I was engaged? I hit my head against the hard rock of the waterfall, hoping it would knock me out enough so that I didn't have to face the stupid, thoughtless, and most erotic thing I'd ever done.

Sugar. Honey. Iced tea. My body was still humming from my orgasm. I mean, when was the last time I'd had one that intense all by myself? Shit, when was the last time I'd had one that amazing with a man? I honestly couldn't remember. It was oh, so freaking hot. The way he watched me, the dirty words, the way he stroked his erection... I think I was a goner from the way he'd kissed me, all-consuming, all-demanding. I was feeling all this sexual need now—what would it be like to have that thick, hard erection inside me? I'd probably faint from joy.

On top of it all, he must have thought I was such a despicable person to do all of this with him when I was actually engaged to be married to another man. Granted, that other man was practically a stranger that I hadn't laid eyes on for nearly a decade, but still, I was off the market and shouldn't be making out—much less masturbating—with another man. Period.

Naseem must think I'm a horrible person.

I attempted to wash away all my thoughts and fears with a little more water from the waterfall, but this time, I found myself hiding behind it like a coward. The waterfall had these grooves where it provided a little shelter, and I stayed behind it to dry off until goosebumps covered my skin and I could no longer prolong facing Naseem. I got dressed in my hoodie and yoga pants and went looking for him.

He had set up an area near the waterfall with branches and leaves in a circle in preparation for a campfire. When I reached him, he was adding more twigs to his pyre. "Want the lighter?"

He glanced up when I approached, but instead of the heat he'd had in his eyes just a few minutes ago, now only coldness greeted me.

"Yeah."

He didn't even look in my direction. He just reached out his hand for my lighter and didn't meet my eyes when he did. "I decided to make camp here because of these big mossy boulders. Now we don't have to sit on the ground."

"I... Oh, good. Thanks."

I was so freaking nervous I couldn't think straight.

The evening sky settled in a misty darkness, making the night darker without the twinkling stars and moonlight. I perched on one of the rocks he had gestured to, and he sat beside me with only the crackling of the fire between us. My heart pounded in my ears. Then, my stomach let out a loud growl, breaking the quiet night.

I was mortified, but he laughed and broke the tension. "Hungry?"

I clutched my stomach. "Yeah, starving."

"Do you still have all those protein bars?"

"Oh, yeah." I reached in my bag and pulled two more out. These really did come in handy. I handed him one and then took the other one for myself.

We sat in silence, but my mind raced. For some reason, I felt the need to rid myself of the guilt I had about Laith. I wanted to confess to Naseem that I actually hadn't spent time with him in over a decade.

"My engagement is arranged."

He stopped chewing and stared at me. "What?"

"Laith's parents and mine are still friends, and they asked for my hand in marriage. He and I barely know each other. Besides one video chat a couple of weeks ago and some messages on Skype, we haven't talked since he followed me to Spain instead of going home after you dumped me."

"Why?" His voice was barely a whisper.

"Why, what? The engagement?"

"Yes, why marry a total stranger?"

I didn't say anything at first, though I knew the answer. I was just too ashamed to admit it.

"Getting married is the last thing to complete my ten-year plan."

"Seriously?"

"What do you want me to say?" I felt my defenses rising. "That I was too broken to fall in love with anyone, so instead of being alone for the rest of my life, I agreed to a marriage to someone who shares my same value system? Wants the same things as me?"

"What's that?"

"Marriage, family, forever."

"How could you possibly want that with someone you don't even love?"

"I fell in love once, and it wasn't worth the heart-break." I got up and walked away. It was too dark to get far from the fire, but seriously, I couldn't be next to him, knowing he was right and I was a total idiot.

I didn't deserve even Laith, because, in truth, I thought I was a horrible person right now, and he deserved better than me. Tears welled in my eyes. I hated that I still felt so much for Naseem. Why couldn't I just be the cold-hearted bitch I needed to be at the moment?

"Summer." The sound of my name on his lips sent trembles down my spine, and my body heated from the inside out. My heart pounded so loud I felt like he could hear it.

"What?" My voice sounded strange to my own ears.

"Come back to the fire."

"I just need a minute."

"No, I don't want to separate at night."

He reached out his hand, and I took it. I was drawn to him like a moth to a flame, and I was tired of fighting it, fighting my emotions.

His hand felt good in my own, surprisingly rough and calloused.

"Why does a pilot have rough hands?"

"I rubbed myself raw under the waterfall."

CHAPTER 9

"So tell me what you've been up to for the last twelve years." We sat side by side on the ground with our backs against the large mossy boulders in front of the massive fire that I'd worked hard to keep going. She handed me another protein bar and took one for herself. "I feel like there is so much about you I don't know anymore."

"Well, after my father died, we sold the store, and I went to the University of Michigan with Carter, studied Aerospace Engineering, and got my pilot's license. I bought my first plane, Jade, and I've been traveling the world since.

"Jade?"

"Yes, that's her name. It's a Bombardier BD-700 1A10. She's still my favorite. But unfortunately, the reason I was able to buy her was that my brother and I inherited my father's insurance money after my mother passed away."

"I'm sure they were happy that it helped you. I think that's what they wanted for you and your brother."

"Sometimes, I feel guilty."

"Why?"

"Because they worked their asses off, opening and closing in that store. Never vacationing, never seeing the world, just working to provide for my brother and I. Then they both died before they even turned forty years old. All that hard work was for nothing. They didn't enjoy anything from their life."

"Is that why you decided to travel for a living, see the world?"

I glanced at her and then wondered how much I should and could share. The truth was, I'd been holding on to these feelings for so long, the words just started to tumble from my lips on their own accord.

"Yeah, I learned from what happened to my parents that life is just too fucking short and I don't want to waste the time I have not enjoying every second of it."

"Your parents' experiences don't mean you'll experience the same things. Thanks to them, you won't have to work fifteen-hour days to try to make ends meet."

"We don't know that we won't experience the same things."

"What do you mean? Your job is different."

"What if I'm destined to die young too?"

"No one knows, but you can't live life from moment to moment. You need to plan for the future."

"That's why you're marrying Laith. Was he part of your grand plan that you keep in your journal?"

"I... Well, yes, getting married is still on that list."

"So the same goal, just different man?" The bitterness in my tone was obvious to my own voice.

"So that explains why I haven't bumped into you in

Michigan. You're never there." She was done having this conversation, her change in topic made it evident.

"Nope. Fly Kakos Airlines is based out of Boston."

"Why Boston?"

"That's where the hangar was when I bought the plane, my brother had just started his residency in a hospital there, and I decided to make that my home base."

"You must be really proud of him. Doctor... Your parents would have been so happy."

"Do you really think our love wasn't worth the time we spent together?"

Her eyes widened and I didn't miss the deep intake of air. She took my hand and placed it in her own, and a feeling of home wrapped around my heart. I hadn't felt those emotions in so long, it was like a part of me awakened the moment she reached for me. We'd kissed and done that sexy game in the waterfall, but this was totally different. Her touch was just for comfort and reassurance, and it hit me straight in the heart. This girl was the love of my life, and the reason I couldn't sit still was that she wasn't by my side.

"Your love, our love was something out of this world, but when you took it away from me, you broke something inside me. Something that I don't think ever mended. So for that reason, for the nights I spent curled in a ball and crying myself to sleep, no, it wasn't worth that pain."

"I'm so sorry." I placed my head on our joined hands in her lap, and my eyes burned with the threat of tears. "I thought I was doing the right thing for you." My voice sounded strange to my own ears. "Summer, *libby*, I was physically sick afterward."

"*Libby*? Don't call me your heart if you don't mean it."

"You will always be my heart," I whispered.

"It wasn't fair for you to take that choice from me." She placed her free hand on top of my head and ran her fingers through my hair, curling the ends of my strands with her fingertips.

"No, it wasn't, and honestly, I think it was the biggest mistake of my life. I wanted you with me. I needed you. Fuck. I still need you. I think I've never stopped needing you."

I lifted my head from her lap and scrubbed my face. I felt like an utter fool. She was going to marry a stranger, and I was professing my undying love for her.

"I never stopped loving you either." She took my face in both hands and kissed the ever-loving lights out of me. She climbed onto my lap, and I wrapped my arms firmly around her waist. It was amazing to have her in my arms—the warmth of her body and the relief of her touch was sending me into overdrive.

I dispensed everything I had into the kiss, every ounce of love and passion that pumped through my veins—I poured it into loving her sweet mouth, kissing her soft, plump lips, and caressing her warm body.

We made out all night, just like when we'd first started kissing when we were horny teens. At the time, she wouldn't let me past second base, so we'd spent hours upon hours kissing, caressing, and a whole lot of clothes burning. Right then, I was reminded of that time, when life was simple and loving someone was enough. We stayed entwined in each other's arms the entire night, and I was completely content with every fucking second of it.

I WOKE UP TO A MASSIVE HARD-ON BENEATH ME AND two hands cupping my ass. Somehow, during one of our make-out sessions last night, I'd straddled him, and the friction was ecstasy between my legs. How long had it been since I'd actually had sex? Six or seven months? I did the math and realized it had been nearly a year. Where had the time gone?

His fingers caressed the waistband of my yoga pants and slid inside. "I fucking love your ass," he whispered. His words, along with his groggy voice in my ear, sent currents of heat right to my core. Well, that and the rod pressed against my most sensitive place.

"Kiss me." He moaned.

"I need to brush my teeth."

"How? Wait, do you have a toothbrush in that magic bag?"

"I have two mini disposable ones."

"Seriously? Why do you have those?"

"I buy them at Target. They're these cute little toothbrushes that you keep in your purse for when you're out and about. It's kind of like a toothpick, but it's a mini brush on one end and a toothpick on the other side."

"Awesome, let's go to the waterfall and wash up. Besides, I have to piss."

At the mention of peeing, my bladder kicked me in the side. I had to pee really bad too, but how the hell was I going to pee in the forest? But I didn't think I could hold it any longer. It had been like fifteen hours, at least. I grabbed my side and started wiggling and leaped off his lap. It was like with just the mention of the P-word, my body was like *yes, we must right now*. "Okay, umm."

"What is it?" He quirked a brow. "Did something bite you?"

"No, I have to pee too."

"So okay, let's do this."

I started to dance around, nearly holding my cookie like I'd seen kids do when they had to go to the bathroom. "I've never peed outside before."

A roar of laughter exploded from him. "You know how cute you look right now? Is that your pee-pee dance?"

"Shut up." I continued to dance in place, holding my side.

"Sweet...*libby*, don't hold it." I thought he was going to call me sweet pea again, but he stopped himself this time. Despite the fact that I was about to explode with the need to relieve myself, my heart couldn't help but glow at him calling me his heart in Chaldean. I was always jealous of the fact he spoke both Arabic and Chaldean. His parents taught him both languages while mine only spoke Arabic with my siblings and me. What little I knew from Chaldean, I'd learned from him.

"Okay, where?"

This way, we'd go together. "No, you can't."

He laughed again. "Are you shy from me, still?"

I did more wiggling. "No, my pee is. This is going to be hard as it is."

"Okay, *libby*, okay. Let's go."

He led me to somewhere close to the waterfall, and the sound of the running water did nothing to ease my need.

"You can't stay," I warned.

He laughed. "Give me the toothbrush, and I'll go to the other side. You can meet me under the waterfall."

He kissed my nose, and the pain was nearly lethal. I

still needed to strip, I mean, what if I got pee on my clothes? I shoved my bag at him and shooed him away.

"Take whatever you want from there and go, now." I started peeling off my clothes, but I turned to find him watching me.

"Why are you still standing here?"

"You're getting naked. How can I possibly leave?"

"Go, please."

"Fine, but don't get dressed when you meet me at the waterfall."

I glared at him but couldn't help the smirk that plastered my face.

When I was finally undressed and had done my thing, I felt so gross, I didn't even want to put my suit bottoms back on, so I didn't.

Instead, I strolled over to the waterfall, butt naked. Naseem was already in the water, and he'd left my fanny pack on the rocks next to his stuff. I dropped my clothes next to his and found the feminine wipes I wanted—I always kept at least one in my purse at all times. I checked, and he wasn't watching, so I slid into the hidden spot from yesterday, brushed my teeth with that disposable toothbrush, and freshened up my lady parts with the wipe. Then, I circled back around the waterfall to rinse my hair.

"Let me do that." His voice behind me sent shivers down my spine. I leaned against his back and let him massage my scalp.

"Give me that sweet mouth."

I moaned before our lips even touched. His fingers slid down my frame, caressing my breasts, circling my nipples, and traveling between my thighs. I trembled in the wake of his skillful hands.

He took his time caressing me, relearning the ways my body responded to his touch. I trembled, holding the rock wall for support, but we'd been teasing our senses all night and I was nearing my explosion. It was only a few strokes of his fingers on my core before my orgasm rocked through me, and I moaned his name.

"Really, is it still that easy to make you come?" he purred in my ear. "Do you remember rubbing my cock against your pussy when you weren't ready to have sex yet?"

"Yes," I moaned.

"Spread your legs and stick out that sexy ass."

He trailed little kisses down my spine, and I yelped at the feel of his lips on the apples of my cheeks.

"What? I happen to remember you telling me yesterday to kiss your ass." His fingers teased against my core and I squirmed.

"I said kiss the beautiful view."

"Sweet pea, that was my beautiful view." His hard cock pressed against my backside and teased my entry. "I was fantasizing what I'd do to this ass all day yesterday." His cock moved between my slick folds, teasing and pleasing all at once. His fingers dug deeper into the apple of my cheek while the other pressed deep inside the core of me. I tossed my head back and released, again.

"Fuck, I want to be inside you. So bad. I want you coming on my dick and calling my name."

"What's stopping you?" I panted.

"Condom. Unless you have one in that magic bag?"

"No." I couldn't get enough of his man, and for once in my life, I didn't think about the consequences of my actions. I turned to face him. Not sure what to do next, I heaved myself up on the rock and spread my legs to make room for him.

"Fuck, you are gorgeous."

"So are you."

I pulled him to me and kissed him hard. My hands roamed his body and reached between us for his erection. He groaned into my mouth. I took my time caressing up and down his shaft. Seriously, it was like when we were teens, exploring each other again, and the love in my heart was still the same as it had been for him then.

When he tossed his head back and climaxed, I loved watching the pleasure on his beautiful face and knowing I'd put it there. He covered my breasts and stomach like he was marking me as his, and my heart squeezed because the reality was, after we left this forest, our little happy bubble was going to shatter.

He washed himself off of me and sadness washed over me. I was going to have to say goodbye to him, this time knowing the truth of why he'd broken my heart.

"What is it?" He brushed my hair from my face and kissed my cheek.

"I'm thinking about when we get back to the villa and it's time for me to get on that plane to Argentina."

I could have stabbed him and he wouldn't have bled. Coldness covered his face and anger radiated from him.

"You're still going to marry Laith? After everything we've shared?"

"I don't know. I thought you were just living in the moment with me, not that you wanted anything more."

"So what was I? Just a last fling, or were you fucking with me to get back at me for the past?"

"No, I wouldn't do that."

"Then what, Summer? What did you expect?"

I stumbled against the rocks, my head spinning from the realization. "You don't want me to get married?"

"No, Summer. I don't. I'm still in love with you. I thought I made that clear yesterday. I thought you wanted the same thing."

"Naseem." I reached for him, but he turned his back to me. I wrapped my arms around his back. "I'm sorry, I thought all that talk about traveling the world and living for today meant just that. You were only living for the day with me right now."

I trailed kisses on his back and shoulder. "Please look at me."

He turned, and I staggered from the sight of his red-rimmed eyes. I took his face in my hands.

"I love you. I've loved you my whole life. Your mother once told me you were the only reason why I didn't cry on the first day of kindergarten. You held my hand and we walked into class our first day together because I was scared."

"She never told me that," he whispered.

"Your mom used to tell me all kinds of things, like how you used to keep my picture under your pillow."

He laughed. "I didn't."

"You did. I found it there once." I tracked the contours of his face with my hands. He leaned into my touch and kissed my fingertips.

"So where does that leave us?"

Where did that leave us? I had no clue. For the first time in twelve years, I felt alive. My reactions had been on autopilot for so many years, and now I was experiencing all the emotions I'd suppressed at once. I gazed into his eyes and love shined back at me. My heart raced. Could I trust his words? I'd believed them once and gotten burned, scorched so badly I'd sworn off love and true intimacy. I was engaged to a virtual stranger because I feared letting anyone into my heart. But in truth, there wasn't room for anyone else because of him. It had always been Naseem, and I knew it deep in my marrow even before I'd gotten on the plane from Detroit to Argentina.

I was still in love with him.

"Together," I whispered.

He smiled wide. "I like the sound of that."

"Me too." I cupped his cheeks. "But Naseem, don't lie or push me away again."

"Never again." He teased my lips with his own. "Now, I need some breakfast before we get back on the trail."

"There are two more protein bars in my bag."

"Oh, no. You're my breakfast." He lifted me up and sat me on the rock again. "Show me that beautiful pussy."

I parted my legs and watched his eyes light up with as much joy as I'd felt in my heart. He caressed my cave and trailed kisses between my parted thighs.

"You smell even better than I remember." He nipped at my entry. "Do you taste the same?"

"Naseem," I pleaded.

"What do you want, sweet pea?"

"You. Always you."

"That's my girl."

CHAPTER 10

"I see something ahead."

After our amazing session in the waterfall, we'd started our trek through the forest. We'd been walking for at least four hours, and the sun and heat were complete killers. But my girl was a trooper, especially since she'd never camped before—at least, not without a camper or bathrooms like at Camp Dearborn, where all the parents from our community would take their families when they finally found time to spend with them.

"A café or restaurant? I'll even eat fast food right now."

"The culinary expert having a fast-food burger, that's desperation."

We were both starving, even though we would have been worse without her protein bars.

"Yes, and some coffee, the deliciously strong Brazilian brew...maybe a creamy pastel or two, oh, or a juicy, mouthwatering cheeseburger..."

"Stop it. My stomach is growling."

The way she described food made my hunger worse, and I was seriously close to eating my arm off.

Then I saw it—the big, bright white high-rise with a hundred balconies.

"That's a hotel." The relief in my voice was evident. I was exhausted and worried because we couldn't spend another night in this place.

She hurried to my side, and I took her hand. It felt good to hold it because it belonged to me.

"Oh my God, I see it. I swear, I could kiss the ground."

"I'd rather you kiss me."

"Honestly, I don't think I'll let you near me until I shower."

"I feel pretty gross too." I pulled her against me anyway and rapped what I could remember from Pitbull and Ying Yang Twins' lyrics from the song "Shake."

She smirked. "Don't quit your day job."

"You swooned when I sang Johnny O's part to you. I know you remembered when I walked into the kitchen."

"You were okay."

"Just okay? I'm pretty sure my voice was the reason you gave up the pussy to me."

"It was. I really felt sorry for you." She pushed away from me and ran for it, giggling, her tight, round ass shaking in that little white bathing suit bottom, making me think of all the things I was going to do to it once I got her on a bed.

"Have I told you, you have one fine ass?"

She looked over her shoulder at me and then flashed me her round rump.

"You keep teasing me like that, just wait, I'm going to claim that ass too."

She stopped running and bent over, holding her knees, which left that fine ass displayed wholly for the taking. I reached her and clasped her hips in my hands and pressed my cock against her ass.

"Stop, freak." She snorted. "This wasn't an invitation."

"Then why in the world did you stop and bend over so perfectly?"

"Because that's the back entrance to the hotel."

I looked up to find the big, spectacular high-rise in its tremendous grand beauty, and relief washed over me.

"Oh, thank you, baby Jesus."

I lifted her off the ground, and she leaped into my arms for a bear hug. "I was beginning to think we weren't going to make it."

"Never again doubt my hiking skills." Something vibrated against my stomach. "Sweet pea, is that your stomach?"

"No, oh, put me down, that's my phone." She quickly rummaged through her bag, taking out her cellphone. "It's Camille."

She hit the green accept button on her home screen and then the speaker button.

"Hey, Camille, thank God," Summer rambled, holding the receiver up to her mouth.

"Seriously, where have you been? I've been worried sick. And if you guys just played hooky to fuck, I'm going to be really pissed."

"What?" Summer rolled her eyes. "No, we had a problem yesterday while hang gliding and we have been lost in the forest."

"Why didn't you answer your phone before now?"

"We didn't have service."

I stepped away to check out where we were. The glorious Rio Rose Hotel looked inviting and like a godsend after the night we'd just had. I left Summer to handle Camille and everyone else while I saw about getting a hotel room, a hot shower, a soft bed, and Summer beneath me.

I gestured for her to follow me. I didn't want to leave her unattended at the back of a hotel, I didn't care how nice it was. She followed while she explained to Camille what had happened to us from the moment the glider tore to our night in the forest. But she conveniently left out the fun and dramatic parts. Once we finally made it to the front entrance, I had Summer wait for me with Camille on the phone as company while I went inside to see about getting a room.

Someone in heaven was smiling down on me when the attractive brunette hotel clerk informed me there was a wedding cancelation and the only thing available was a honeymoon suite. I threw up another prayer of thanks when I found my credit card and ID were in my pants unharmed—three fucking cheers for zipper pockets in jogging pants. I explained our situation, and the receptionist was eating out of my hands. She assisted me with ordering room service and promised that it would be brought up to our room as soon as possible.

After I'd made a quick trip to the hotel drugstore for condoms, I found us each Rio T-shirts, shorts, and flip-flops to change into on the way back to the villa tomorrow, because tonight, clothes were absolutely not required. I found Summer right where I'd left her, still chatting with Camille.

"Hey." Her face lit up when I returned holding a hotel key card and two water bottles. "Umm, Cammy, we are actually going to stay at this hotel tonight, and we will be back in the morning for the wedding."

"Bye, Camille," I teased and heard her chuckle just as I ended the call.

Summer accepted the water bottle from me and took a long pull. Water tinkled down her neck and onto her bikini top, hitting the spot right above her nipple. My cock twitched in my pants.

"You were just in time. She was grilling me about us."

"She can wait and grill you tomorrow, because right now, I'm about to nail you." I flashed her the inside of my bag and showed her the condoms. Her cheeks turned the perfect shade of pink I loved, and she did that sexy nibble on her bottom lip.

"That's a big box."

"It's going to be a really, really long night."

"Is sex the only thing you think about?" She arched a brow.

"No, not only sex. I think about flying too. Have you ever joined the mile-high club?"

"Still sex."

"Have you?"

"No."

"Well, we are adding that to our to-do list."

"We have a to-do list?"

"Yeah. I know how much you like them, so I figured we'd make one of our own."

She kissed my cheek. "You can be really sweet when you want to be."

"Just you wait. You'll see what a giver I really am."

She batted her lashes. "I'm looking forward to it."

There were so many things I wanted to share with her. So many experiences I'd had that I wished would've been with my girl. I didn't just want to do those things for her—I wanted them for me. She was everything to me. Something had happened in that forest. I couldn't explain it—maybe it was learning that our breakup had been just as painful for her as it was for me, or maybe seeing her nearly drown twice, or the way her laugh filled me with a sense of coming home. Despite my fears of my own mortality, I knew without a shadow of a doubt I wanted to live every moment I had left on this earth with her.

Taking the key card from my hand, she exited the elevator, and I happily followed like a lovesick puppy. It was a good thing this was a beach hotel, or we would have looked pretty silly walking around in our bathing suits.

"Wait, is this a honeymoon suite?" She pointed at the heart-shaped rose petals sprinkled on the king-size bed.

"Yeah, it was the only room left."

"Nice." She took off her Nikes at the door. "I want to toss these in the garbage."

"You can. I picked you up some flip-flops from the store."

"Really? What else did you get?"

"Clothes, but you aren't getting these until tomorrow."

"Tomorrow?"

"You won't need them tonight."

"That's really presumptuous."

"Don't you want to stay, Summer?" I stalked toward her. She backed away and pressed her body against the hall. I hovered over her, my mouth just inches from hers, my stare burning into wide eyes. Her breath hitched, and she licked her lips.

"There isn't anywhere else I'd rather be."

"Show me." She pulled me back and went into the

luxurious bathroom with double marble sinks, white marble floors, a standing shower big enough for me to lie down in, and a massive jet tub in the center.

She undid her bikini top and let it fall to the ground. Next, her bottoms came off, and she stepped out of them.

There was a knock and someone calling, "Room service," at the door.

She did that sex laugh I just loved, all throaty and so seductive. "You better get that, unless you want me to go like this?"

I think I almost growled at her words.

"Okay, I guess not."

I tried not to laugh at her teasing me, but I chuckled all the way to the door. Letting the guy bring in the carts and tipping him was a bit of a struggle because my cash was a little stuck together. When he finally left, I made my way into the bathroom.

Steam covered everything, and I could just make out her lush shape behind the foggy glass. I undressed and noticed the toothbrushes on the counter, side by side. My heart did this weird flutter, and I began to question my manhood. She'd already unwrapped one of the complimentary toothbrushes, and I helped myself to the other one. After taking care of business, I took my shorts off and placed them in a heap next to hers.

I slid the shower door open and entered the steam-filled square of space. Water was streaming out at every angle, and I took a few seconds to savor the rush of the hot water on my skin.

She turned to look at me, her body all lathered and wet, her glorious nipples peeking through the soapsuds, foam tracing her stomach and the little patch of hair between her legs. My mouth went dry. I mean, I'd seen her basically naked all weekend, but something about this moment—maybe because I was only a few moments away from finally having her—made my whole body tremble with anticipation.

"Hi." Her eyes combed over my body. "Need some soap?"

I couldn't find my words, so I just nodded my head. I watched as she took the washcloth and lathered it with body wash.

"Would you like me to wash you?"

I nodded again, still finding it hard to express this emotion in my chest. She sauntered over to me. Slowly, she dragged the washcloth over my chest, stomach, and arms, leaving little trembles in her wake. Her eyes never leaving my own until she circled me to wash my back, ass, and legs. Every stroke of that washcloth made me madder with lust. Finally, she was in front of me, and I reached for her—but she pulled away.

"I'm showing you there's no other place I'd rather be."

Her little hands washed my chest again, then lingered above my cock, but she slid past and washed my thighs and calves, working her way between my legs. My body shuddered, and I dug my nails into my palms to keep myself from reaching for her again.

She pressed me against the shower door and lathered her hands. When she touched my balls, I nearly buckled. That vixen knew what she was doing to me. She grinned widely and worked her hand over my cock while water poured over our heads. Then her sweet mouth was on me, and it wasn't long before I lost control. It was the fastest blast-off I'd ever had, and I think it was from all the anticipation. I attempted to pull away, but she gripped me tighter, taking me deeper, and when I peaked, she took all of me.

~

My body thrummed with desire. I didn't think I'd ever tire of watching him climax. He was so beautiful and powerful. I loved how he tried so hard to keep eye contact and the way he moaned my name when he finished—so powerful. So magnificent to watch a strong man unravel because of something I was doing.

He pulled me to my feet and kissed me hard on the mouth, his hands roaming all over my body before finding home between my legs. It was only a few strokes of his magical fingers in the right spot and I climaxed.

"You come so quickly for me. I want to taste you."

My stomach let out the loudest hungry cry of its life. The roaring noise echoed the shower stall, and I froze in mortification.

"Was that your stomach?" He laughed, and I hid my head in his chest and giggled from pure embarrassment.

"Yes, I'm starving."

"Come on, let's feed you. You're going to need your strength for what I have in store for you."

After drying off and getting dressed in hotel white fluffy bathrobes, we made our way to the food cart he had ordered for us.

The tray was covered with burgers, fries, chicken tenders, tacos, and even the pastry treats I'd been craving this afternoon.

"I know it's been a while since we've eaten, but babe, that's a lot of food."

"You called me babe." He wiggled his eyebrows at me.

I rolled my eyes and shoved a handful of French fries in my mouth.

"I'm warning you," I said between bites, "nothing about the way I'm going to eat right now is going to be ladylike."

"I love a girl who can eat."

I took a giant bite of the hamburger and chewed like a madwoman, not even caring about manners. "So good."

"Summer."

"Hmm." I took another bite, almost making love to the burger.

"Marry me."

CHAPTER 11

Did he just ask me to marry him?

Naseem Kakos just asked me to marry him, holy moly guacamole.

My heart leaped, it soared, but it immediately crashed and burned at the surprised look on his face. He hadn't meant to ask me.

"Summer, I..."

"You don't have to say anything. You were just captivated by my charm and skills in the shower. You don't have to explain. We can pretend it never happened."

"What? No."

He walked over to me, but I kept my burger that I just realized I'd been clutching to my chest firmly between us like a barrier.

"Are you saying that you were planning on asking me to marry you, right at this moment?"

"Well, no, but I was just watching you, and I needed to put a ring on it before you try to marry any more strangers." He kissed my cheek and returned to the chair where he'd been sitting before he dropped the M-bomb.

"Dirty." I rolled my eyes and busied myself with my hamburger because I didn't have the guts to look at him.

"It doesn't change the fact that I still really want you to be mine."

I didn't answer him. My face steamed with heat from the inside out. Even in my moments of denial, I'd always dreamed of this moment. Naseem groveling, telling me he had always loved me and couldn't spend another moment without me. Though it all didn't happen the way I had pictured, it had happened, and instead of climbing into his lap and shouting *yes, yes, yes*, I was riddled with fear and doubt.

"Sweet pea."

I placed the burger on the cart and made my way over to him. Something in the way he called me that melted me deep inside to my core. I stood before him. He spread his legs for me to fit between his thighs. His white terrycloth robe split and displayed the hard muscles of his chest and thighs. His arms wrapped around my hips and cupped my bottom.

"Look at me." Our eyes met, and the love I saw in them was staggering. I cupped his face, and he leaned into my touch. Trembles slid down my spine when he kissed my palm.

"Look, I know you think you want to marry me, but since it was just a thought that popped into your mind after I gave you head, I really want you to think about it long and hard, then you can ask me again."

"Fine. If you need time to process, I'll give it to you."

"I just want you to be sure."

He smacked my behind. "Finish that burger and get your strength together. We still have a box of condoms to get through."

I laughed. "You plan on using the whole box tonight?"

"Absolutely."

I curled up in the chair beside his and finished eating my burger and fries and stewed in my thoughts. It was crazy. I'd wanted him to think about his impromptu proposal, but now I was obsessing about if and when he was going to ask again, and that might not be for some time, if ever. What was I thinking, anyway? I was technically still engaged—well, until I broke it off tomorrow. I was sure Laith would understand; it was my parents that were going to be the problem. I could hear my mom now. *"You are going to humiliate us. You can't back out now, we gave our word."*

But honestly, all of that wouldn't matter if I truly had Naseem back in my life. All of it would be worth it.

I woke with Naseem's arms wrapped around me in a white plush bed. The last thing I remembered was sitting in that blue chair. The sun had faded, and the moon radiated through the open balcony. I was burning hot with the bathrobe and Naseem's body heat against me. I attempted to pull away, but his hands gripped me tighter.

"Where do you think you're going?" The gruff sound of his voice was like a mating call to my lower body.

"I'm hot."

He nipped my ear. "Yeah, you are."

I giggled like a schoolgirl. "No, I mean this robe is hot. I need to take it off."

He leaped off of me. "I have no problem with you getting naked."

"I bet you don't." I turned to face him. He was completely naked from the waist up and he looked delectable in the moonlight. My eyes roamed his body and the way the sheet bunched up around his waist.

"I love the way you look at me when you're horny." His low, rumbling laugh made my stomach flutter in anticipation.

I got off the bed and made my way to the bathroom, but not before calling over my shoulder at him, "Take a look in the mirror, Pilot Kakos. You're pretty damn sexy when you want to get some action."

After washing my face and doing my business, I came out to a room filled with candlelight. Naseem was gloriously naked and holding one red rose.

"What's this?" I breathed.

"Look, while you were sleeping, I did what you asked and thought about us and what I wanted."

He reached out his hand for me, and I nearly floated over to him. He clasped our fingers together, and his warm lips touched my fingertips with a soft caress.

"I know that I love you. I know that I'm crazy about you. I know you're the only girl I've ever loved. The only girl I will ever love. Life is short. We don't know what tomorrow is going to bring, but I know if I only have a few minutes in this life, I want them with you."

My heart was pounding in my ears, his words nearly muffled by the sound of my rushing pulse. He got on one knee in front of me.

"I'm naked before you, baring my soul. Marry me, Summer. I don't want another sunrise or sunset without you in my arms."

Tears were gushing from my eyeballs. I cupped his face and kissed him as if I needed him to breathe. In a lot of ways, I didn't think I'd exhaled properly in twelve years. The lack of him in my life was highlighted now that he was back, and that realization scared the crap out of me. Was I truly not alive without him?

He lifted me into his arms, and I wrapped my legs around his waist. He tore his lips away. "Was that a yes, Summer?"

"Yes. Yes. Yes." I punctuated each word with a hard kiss against his laughing lips.

He placed me on the bed and covered me with his body. The luscious naked weight and strength of him were welcomed by my growing need to have him. I arched my back and let our bare bodies caress. I moaned to the feel of his hard form against my softer curves.

His lips teased my neck, my ear, and moved to my breasts. Every flick of his wicked tongue drove me deeper to the edge of wild.

"Naseem."

"Hmmm." He licked, nibbled, and sucked. Teasing me with every slash of his tongue.

"I need you inside."

"Are you wet for me, Summer?"

"Yes."

"I'll have to check first."

He made his way down my body, leaving playful kisses in his wake. He spread my legs and pressed his face between my thighs.

"You smell so good."

His unshaven face teased my sensitive skin, and my body trembled with need.

"That's right," he mumbled from between my legs, "ride my face."

"Naseem." I grabbed handfuls of his hair and pulled.

Warm air kissed my core as he chuckled. "I need to hear the words. Tell me what you want."

"Make me come."

"Fuck." That was the last coherent word I remembered him saying because he devoured me. Every part of me hummed in pleasure. He lapped, sucked, and warmed my whole body. I sensed him everywhere. Heat and pleasure washed around me and settled in my core and coiled. I heard his moans of gratification while he pleasured me. My world tilted, my body soared, and my climax crashed down on me in a heap of bliss.

I heard the rustling of the condom wrapper, and a fluttery sensation twirled in my chest. I got on my knees and watched him stroke his shaft in the candlelight.

"How do you want me?"

"Fuck. Sweet pea, give me that mouthwatering ass."

I turned around and planted my hands on the mattress, spreading my legs and raising my bottom in the air. "Like this?"

"Don't move."

I felt the bed shift and he climbed behind me. His warm hands gripped my hips, and he pressed his erection against my butt cheeks. He positioned his hand flat on my back and the other between my legs.

"I'm going to go hard and fast right now. But I promise the next time will be slow."

His fingers teased my entry.

"Naseem."

"You know I need to hear it from you, sweet pea."

"Fuck me." I pushed my rear back into his erection. "Now."

Before I could say anything else, his erection was at my entrance, and my mouth went dry. His finger worked my clit but I was so wet that when I bucked against him, I pushed him into me. My breath hitched from the sheer invasion of him inside of me. He rocked into me with a wild and wicked abandon. He'd requested this position because he'd wanted to claim me, and with every stroke, he was making me his. And I'd asked him because I wanted him to.

He was right. Our lovemaking was hard, fast, and messy. My head banged into the headboard—thank goodness it was tufted, and this time, when I climaxed, he flipped me on my back, lifted my leg over his shoulder, and claimed me again, but this time slowly.

I closed my eyes and let the feel of him take me to places my body hadn't been in a long time.

"Fuck, yes, touch yourself." I opened my eyes to find that my hands were caressing my breasts on their own accord while he gave me pleasure with his body. I looked him directly in the eyes and let my hands roam down to my clit, and he moaned.

"Feed me." He slowed down his pace even more, each stroke of his erection slow and deliberate. I circled my clit with my index finger and lifted it to his lips.

He licked my finger with careful, loving thrashes of his wicked tongue. With the combination of his slow, sensual, and steady movements, and the erotic feel of my finger in and out of his mouth, my body convulsed, and a wicked orgasm exploded through me. This time, I brought him with me.

He kissed down my body before he withdrew, and I hated the emptiness afterward. I loved the feel of him inside me. It gave me this symbolic sense that we would be joined together forever. After he cleaned up, he held me to him.

"I love when I get you to say the word *fuck*. I'm pretty sure I've gotten you to say it like three times."

. . .

"WHEN?" I DIDN'T REMEMBER SAYING THE F-WORD. I didn't like swearing—that was why I always used food words instead.

"Just now." He caressed one nipple and nibbled behind my ear. "When you asked me to fuck you."

"I don't remember." My face heated. I remembered, but I refused to admit it.

He rolled me onto his chest in a bear hug and my legs wrapped around his. "Give me that sweet mouth." And on command, I kissed him. With all the passion and desire I had for him, I kissed him.

"Summer," he panted.

"Hmm?" I teased his bottom lip.

"I'm going to fuck you again, but first, let's call room service."

"You really know the way to my heart is through my stomach."

"Yes. It was the way you ate that hamburger that made me want to marry you."

"Really? Not the blowjob in the shower?

"Why, I don't know, you might have to do it again so I can decide fairly."

I moved my hand down his shaft and cupped his sack. He was hard already. "It's a deal."

I scooted off him and went to the phone on the nightstand.

"What do you want?"

"Ice cream."

"Ice cream? I thought you wanted real food."

"Order me a steak, medium, with whatever side, but I also want ice cream."

"Chocolate still your favorite?"

"You remembered."

"I did."

I flipped through the menu. "Okay, the ice cream comes in either a waffle cone or bowl."

"You pick. I won't be eating it from the cone or bowl."

"Then how will you eat it?"

"Ever play with your food, sweet pea?"

~

THE INSISTENT RINGING PULLED ME OUT OF THE BEST sleep I'd ever had in my life.

"Who is calling us?" I groaned.

"What time is it?" Summer wigged beneath me but I held her tighter, refusing to let her go.

"I think we're late."

"We still have more condoms."

"You're so insatiable."

I pressed my dick against her ass cheek. "I still didn't get inside here."

"And you're not. That's a no-entry zone."

The phone rang again, and she pushed me off with a little more force. I pouted like a little kid but still enjoyed watching her naked ass get out of bed to answer the phone.

"Hello." She spoke into the receiver with her eyes on me, so I decided to give her a little show. I pulled back the sheet and let my cock stand tall and proud.

"Hi, Camille." She hit a button on the phone and watched me with a wicked stare. Camille's voice echoed in our private little room.

"Where the hell are you guys?"

"We overslept. What time is it?" The humor in her tone evaporated.

"Only eleven a.m. You have about an hour to get your cute butts down here for the ceremony."

"I thought they already had one in Australia?"

"They did, but my mom is insisting that she see her only baby boy take his vows with the love of his life. You know my mom. Now get one more quickie in and get your asses down here."

"Camille, I love you," I yelled from my side of the bed.

Summer just laughed and covered her face. "Bye, Camille."

When Summer hung up the phone, she watched me with fire-filled eyes, her nakedness illuminated by the sunlight streaming in from behind her.

"What are you looking at, Summer?"

"The man I love." Her cheeks blushed the cutest shade of pink.

"Come make love with your man." I opened my arms and beckoned her. She floated over to me and cradled my hips between her thighs. This time she reached for the condom and fumbled as she placed it over my shaft.

"Ride your man," I whispered.

She got on her knees and angled my cock against her entry, taking all of me to the hilt. I held her hips and guided her up and down my length. Her heat was so warm and sweet. This was coming home. I'd forgotten the feel of belonging, the sense that someone was a part of you, until the very moment I'd realized I'd been homeless all this time. Despite the money, fancy planes, and vacations, I was empty and hollow because she wasn't with me.

She moaned and closed her eyes, her beautiful tits swaying with every thrust of her hips. I sat up to meet her and tasted the sweet, salty skin behind her ears. She clapped my shoulders, searing pain from her fingernails dug into my back, and her pace quickened.

She was an amazing sight, and my orgasm was coming, but I wasn't coming alone. I slid my fingers between her legs, and she quivered against my hand.

"Your pussy is so wet."

"Yes." She moaned, tossing her head back. Her movements were messy and losing coordination.

"You like taking control, don't you?"

"Yes..." She bit her lip and tilted over my body to kiss me. With a few more flicks of my fingers on her clit, she was spiraling out of control. Her orgasm hit her hard and triggered my own. Sill nestled inside her, I cradled her body to me. This was home. Her in my arms. Home sweet home.

CHAPTER 12

"Seriously, you guys are wearing matching outfits?" Camille was the first one to spot us when we entered the villa. "How high school."

"We need to change."

"Well, yes, unless the best man wants to stand at the altar in Rio swag."

"How much time do we have?"

"Umm, like ten minutes."

Naseem kissed my forehead and headed to his room to change his clothes.

"You look adequately fucked."

I laughed. "You have no idea."

"I might if it runs in the family." Camille giggled.

We rushed to Camille's room, and I changed into a lavender summer dress. She helped me tame my mane of curls with a few sprays of salt water and a little curling cream. I didn't have time for a blow-dry, so I fully embraced curly girl. After lathering up on moisturizer—my face felt so dry from the lack of products for the last few days—I did my make-up in record time. Thanks to the time in the sun, I was sun-kissed and didn't need to put on too much.

We made it out only a few minutes late. The patio door was open, and a white linen path led to a rose-covered arch, creating the most beautiful altar and framed by a few white folding chairs on each side.

Rahim and Carter's mom and dad were already sitting in the chairs, waiting.

"I have to check on Corinne—she's the flower girl."

I nodded at Camille and made my way down the aisle to take my seat.

"Oh my goodness, I'm so glad you're okay." Camille's mom leaped up and pulled me into the biggest bear hug. "We were worried sick about you."

"Yeah, that was definitely an adventure."

"I told those two that the adventures have to stop. They aren't reckless boys anymore."

"They were reckless, huh?"

"Oh yes, they were complete terrors. Every chance they got, they were off jumping out of planes and learning to ride every flying contraption under the sun." She pushed away a strand of her golden hair from her face. "Yeah, you know, they both were fighting demons, and the crazy stuff was their way of testing their own mortality, I suppose."

"You think they still do?"

"Carter changed with Kendall. Hopefully, so will Naseem now that he's with you. And don't worry, dear, Camille told me all about how he won your heart. Of course, I still don't understand why you were going to marry a man you barely know. But I'm glad you are calling it off."

My face burned hot. "Umm, yeah, well, I hope my family is as understanding as you are."

"Is your mother going to be cross?"

"Well, it was a traditional wedding arrangement made by the parents. I'm pretty sure my mother will be livid."

"Now, you're the same ethnicity as Naseem?"

"Yeah, both of us are first-generation Assyrian-Chaldean born in the US."

"From Iraq, right?"

"Yup. Mom and Dad's families migrated here in the 70s."

"And their marriages were arranged?"

"You can say that, but really, my parents were at the same event, and my father met my mom and liked her, and his mother called and asked for my mother's hand in marriage the next day."

"Did your mom have a say?"

"Well, yes, they asked her if she wanted to. She said my father was attractive, made her laugh, came from a good family, and would be a good provider, so she agreed."

"That's lovely that they were able to make the relationship work even though they were basically strangers."

"Yeah, my mother said the love came later, afterward."

Love came later. Was that what I'd expected to happen if I'd gone through with the arranged marriage? Thinking about it now, I didn't think so. I refused to fall in love with Laith because, until my little adventure with Naseem in the forest, I'd felt that love was too much of a risk.

Yet Mrs. Clynes's words resonated with me. It was true my parents had made it work, not out of love, but out of basic understanding, a whole lot of giving and taking, faith, and trust. But was that enough? Camille took her seat next to me just as the music started to chime.

Naseem walked down the aisle first. He wore tan linen pants, a white button-down shirt, and bare feet. He looked so delicious, and I wondered if I could possibly ever love him more. He stood to the right of the aisle, our eyes met, and he beamed at me. The love and devotion shone in his features.

Carter made his way down, wearing a similar look to Naseem, except his pants were white linen. He was happy and beamed with love as he glanced at his mom.

Next, little Christopher and Corinne walked down together, Corinne in a pink summer dress and leaving pink rose petals behind her.

"Oh my goodness."

"Aren't my grandchildren the cutest?"

"Oh, yes, and so smart. I want my kids to be just like them."

"I'm so glad you talked Naseem out of that silly notion, then."

"What notion?"

"That he didn't think he was fit to have children."

My heart raced. What the hell did that mean, not fit to have children? How could someone want to get married but not have children?

"I didn't know that was even a notion."

"Oh, I... It was probably just some silly boy ideas. You know, men grow and change."

I could tell this conversation was making her uncomfortable, and honestly, I felt like a dumpling-head, so I just kept my jaws closed. But the unease in my chest wasn't something easily dismissed.

"Oh, Cat looks lovely."

She cooed over her daughter and I let her. Catherine, also wearing pink, looked stunning as ever, walked down the aisle and stood to the left of the altar. But it was Kendall who was breathtaking and looked like a movie star. Her white silk gown poured like liquid on her tiny frame and also swayed with her as she came down the aisle on the arm of a dashing Mr. Clynes. But instead of watching Kendall, my gaze drifted to Carter, and the love I saw in his eyes made my heart swell.

Carter clasped hands with his father and embraced him before linking fingers with Kendall. It was the first time I'd noticed the striking resemblance between the two men. Both Carter and his father had the same handsome features, muscular frame, and dark hair, but it was their charisma that made them attractive.

I glanced in Naseem's direction and his eyes were on me. The intensity in his spoke volumes of his love for me. I smiled. The tension in my body released, and I exhaled a breath. I had nothing to worry about. He must have changed his mind about family because he'd changed his mind about relationships and marriage. Children had to be on the top of that list too.

He mouthed, "I love you," and my heart blossomed and rejoiced. This man, the man I'd loved my whole life, even when I'd wanted to forget, to stop, was always in my heart, and right now, this man stood in front of me, tall, strong, and completely at ease with his love for me. He was confident in us, and I had to be too.

Carter had arranged for a minister from the local church to do the ceremony, and it was beautiful.

"Since the bride and groom have already had their official wedding in Australia, they decided that they would read their own vows for this ceremony. Carter, you first," the minister said.

"I, Carter, promise to dream with you, laugh with you, support you, and tell you I love you every day. I promise to send you dirty text messages when I'm away and ask before I steal your panties and always help you lift stains off your shirts, even if I didn't cause them."

Kendall covered her mouth and blushed ten shades of red, but Carter flashed us all a mischievous grin. We all chuckled, and she smiled shyly, but her eyes glinted with joy.

Tears ran down my cheeks and my chest squeezed. An apprehension filled me. What if Naseem didn't want children? Would I never have this moment with him? Would that be a deal-breaker for me? My pulse raced and my mouth went dry.

Carter flashed us a grin and continued. "My Perky, I promise to love you with my actions, not just my words, but in every task in our daily lives. I promise to wash the dishes if you dry, I promise to vacuum if you dust, and I promise to make the bed if you lie with me every night. I promise to make every moment of our lives a partnership because even the mundane tasks are exciting when I'm sharing them with you. You are my partner and friend for life, and I promise to forever love and honor you."

Kendall dabbed her eyes with a tissue Catherine handed her before speaking. "Carter, from the moment we met, you surprised and captivated me. You challenged me and encouraged me to follow my heart, and I promise to always be grateful you spilled your drink on my designer blouse. I, Kendall, vow to pretend not to notice when you eat off my plate. I promise to not get jealous of the endless women who cook for you and pamper you, as long as they stay over the age of sixty-five."

Camille cackled beside me.

"Over sixty-five?" I whispered.

"Carter used to live in a senior citizen community. Long story." She grinned.

"I promise to laugh at all your corny music jokes even when they're not funny. I promise to never go to sleep angry and never wear a bra whenever I can help it. I promise you endless red-light specials, moonlight swims, and countless adventures. I promise to follow you to the moon and stars if you ask me to. You are my guide, my light, and my every wish, and I promise to love and honor you, always and forever."

Camille grabbed my shoulder. "Now those are the kinds of vows I want in my life, except 'nightly orgasm' would be added to mine," she whispered only for me to hear, and I muffled a giggle.

"These promises might be trivial to some, but they are going to be the way this beautiful couple confirms their love for each other every day. Words are only words, but the little acts, the small practical tasks, are the promise of love and the foundation of relationships. You see, it's the sacrifices we make every day for each other that builds a life, that creates a family," the minister said.

I didn't realize it, but tears were pouring down my face. I watched as they exchanged rings and kissed under the altar of flowers. We all cheered, clapped, and tossed more rose petals at them. Joy and happiness radiated from the lovely family that surrounded me, and warmth wrapped around my heart like a loving blanket. The beautiful couple laughed and cheered along with us. We all made our way to them, each giving our well wishes.

"Congratulations." I hugged Kendall. "You look beautiful. I love this dress."

"Thank you, I love it too. You know, you always hear about how people just get that feeling when they find their wedding dress. I didn't believe it, but then I tried this on and swooned."

"I swooned when I saw her in this dress." Carter put his arms around his blushing bride. "She looks fucking fantastic."

"She most certainly does." I hugged him. "Thank you so much for sheltering me while I was stranded."

"I'm just so glad we actually bumped into you. I'd hate the thought of you being alone this whole time while we're in the same place," Carter said.

"Me too." Naseem slipped his arms around my waist and pulled me close. "It's like the chick flick, *Serendipity*."

We all turned to look at him with the same puzzled expressions.

"*Serendipity*?" Carter asked.

"Yeah, you know, that movie where the girl believes in fate and shit." Naseem tucked my head under his chin and wrapped me into a tighter embrace.

"Oh yeah, she writes her name and phone number in a book, and if he finds the book, then they were meant to be together," Kendall said.

"Right, but it's crazy, like it takes a few years for it to happen," Naseem said.

Carter and I stared at each other in disbelief, and at the same time, we exploded in laughter.

"What's so funny?" Naseem wobbled me in his arms.

"The fact that you're quoting chick flicks." Carter chuckled.

"I watched chick flicks in high school. Where do you think I learned my game from?"

"What game?" I laughed.

"You think you're funny, huh?" He nipped at my ear.

"I'm hilarious." I lightly elbowed him and he released his hold. "You did have a few really good moves, but I thought they were original."

"Not all of them were from the movies."

"I think it's sweet," Kendall said.

"And the bride is always right," Carter said, and we all agreed. "Come on, Perky, let me get you some champagne."

After the photographer took pictures of the bride and groom, Carter insisted on all of us taking group pictures to remember the occasion.

"Who would have thought Carter was such a sap?" Naseem pulled me in for a longing hug.

"It's cute, actually. This is a family time they all will never forget."

"How about one of the two of you?" The photographer, Selena, smiled broadly, her dark brown hair dancing in the ocean breeze.

"Sure." Naseem tucked me tightly against his body, and I posed for the camera.

"Beautiful," Selena said.

Naseem kissed my cheek. "Yes, she is."

"Yes, and you make a beautiful couple. Bless you."

My face flushed hot and I thanked Selena.

After the pictures, we all settled into the beautiful tablescape for a lovely, intimate setting for the family, plus Rahim—he might've been getting closer to Camille than any of us had thought—and Naseem and me.

"Summer, come play with me. You promised a game

of Go Fish when you got back, and you are totally late," Corinne scolded me with a pack of playing cards in hand.

"Yes ma'am," I said.

We played a few hands before Christopher came over and wanted to join.

"We should play boys against girls," Christopher said.

"Umm, you are the only boy. You need another boy on your team," Corinne said.

"I have one." Christopher waved his hand, and Naseem appeared as though he'd orchestrated the whole thing.

"Have room for one more?"

"Yeah, boys against girls. Remember? It was your idea," Christopher said, a little exasperated. "Don't you remember?"

"I do, little buddy, but did you miss the part about it being our little secret?"

"He doesn't know how to keep a secret," Corinne said. "Last year, he spoiled grandma's birthday surprise."

"I did not."

"Did too."

"All right, how about we start that game of Go Fish?" I said.

"Yeah, how about we start." Corinne mimicked my tone, and Naseem and I glanced at each other, laughing. After three rounds of Go Fish, the girls beat the boys 3-0.

"I want a rematch," Christopher insisted.

"Maybe later, sweetheart. I think it's time to get some lunch." Camille and Catherine were waving the kids over.

"Okay."

"They are awesome. I can't wait until we have some of our own." The words were out of my mouth before I could stop them, but Naseem ignored my comment entirely.

"Hungry?"

"Starving," I lied.

And just like that, I lost my appetite, even though I had been famished only a few moments ago.

"Let's get some food." I stood from my chair and smoothed down my dress. The wind was picking up, and I was doing a whole lot of Marilyn Monroe.

"Did I tell you how beautiful you look?"

"Only once or twice." I laughed, but it was fake to my own ears. Carter's mom's voice echoed in my head. *"He didn't think he was fit to have children."*

Pushing the negative thoughts from my mind, I focused on him. He hadn't rejected the idea of children, and I had to hope his silences meant he was in agreement of having a few of our own.

Lunch on the patio was in full swing. Even though Camille and I had planned to cook for the event since it was just a few of us, Carter hadn't allowed it—he'd already catered the entire evening with hors d'oeuvres, lunch, and dinner with servers so Maria Rosa could enjoy the celebration along with everyone.

"Did you want me to make you a plate?" I asked Naseem.

"I don't think I've had anyone make me a plate since my mom."

"Well, that's going to change. You know how much I love to cook."

"I don't think I'm hungry for food anymore."

"Yeah, I think they have sweets too, besides the wedding cake."

"Nope, I'm only hungry for your sweets."

Heat rose in my cheeks. Despite the need to be as close as possible to him right now, I couldn't bring myself to play along.

"You can taste tonight. You are the best man, remember?"

"Yes, I remember. Got my speech ready and everything," Naseem said.

"It's time for the best man's speech." Camille clinked her fork against her glass, and Naseem rose, his usual cocky demeanor dialed back, and if I wasn't mistaken, he was actually really shy.

"I'm not sure where to begin, so I'll start with the family I feel I've gained through my friendship with Carter. The Clynes bunch is a really welcoming group—yes, even you, Camille."

We all laughed.

"I want to thank you all for taking me in all those years ago. Inviting me to spend holidays at your home when I wasn't even sure where home was for me anymore. Sending me care packages along with Carter's when we were in college and cheering on my achievements like they were your own."

Mrs. Clynes wiped her eyes.

"Along the way, you became my family and he became a brother. So I have to know, Carter Clynes, how did you trick such a beautiful woman into marrying you?" Everyone at the table giggled except Mrs. Clynes, who mumbled something about her baby boy being very gorgeous.

"Seriously, Kendall, how did he do it?" Naseem laughed, then lifted his hands in surrender. "Kidding, just kidding. You guys are perfect together—you laugh together, play together, and most importantly, the two of you bring out the best in each other. You both light up around the other. Some would say you're soulmates, but you don't only seem to be soulmates. Instead, it feels like you are created from the same bright and shiny star." He lifted his glass. "To Carter and Kendall, may you always be each other's light. All together now; all you need is love."

The laughter that erupted startled me. His speech was really sweet, all of it. My heart ached for him when he described the feeling of not knowing where home actually was anymore. Naseem and Carter embraced, and Carter mentioned something about the Beatles song titles.

"What's so funny?" I asked Camille.

"Naseem used two Beatles song titles at the end of his speech. 'All Together Now' and 'All You Need Is Love.'"

"Wait, what?"

"Yes, Carter has this thing—he says there's a Beatles song title for every situation. And Nas just used two of them for him."

"Why didn't you ever tell me how close he was with your family?"

Camille surveyed me for a moment and then sighed. "I tried once. Do you remember me mentioning him to you after we got home from Spain?"

"I think I blocked much of it out of my mind."

"I didn't forget. You scared the living shit out of me."

There were still parts of that night that were wiped from my memory because I'd blacked out completely after I'd given myself alcohol poisoning and gone home with a random stranger.

"I'm sorry. I still can't believe I was that irresponsible."

"I'm just glad that dude wasn't a creeper or even worse."

Actually, he was a really nice guy, didn't take advantage of me, and got in touch with his friend so he could call Camille. I was such a hot mess when she got there that she freaked and took me to the hospital to get my stomach pumped—and to make sure I hadn't been sexually assaulted.

"So yeah, after that reaction, I didn't ever want to say his name around you again."

"I get it. I just wish I'd known about his family. He went through so much. I'm really glad he had you guys. I think you might be a family of superheroes."

Music started. The words "And I Love Her" blared from the little boom box in Maria's living room, and the happy couple began dancing with so much love my stomach knotted. The way Carter and Kendall looked at one another was what I'd found again with Naseem, but I was terrified of losing it. I still couldn't forget what Mrs. Clynes had said about him not wanting children, and his intentional dodge of my comment about us having kids.

"'And I Love Her'—that's another Beatles song. My brother is nothing if not predictable."

"Mama, I want to dance." Corrine came over and climbed into Camille's lap. "But Christopher won't dance with me."

"Do you want to dance with Mama and Summer?"

Her bright blue eyes lit up. "Yes, that would be so fun."

Though I really didn't feel up to it, I took Corrine's empty hand and started dancing. Somehow, the music changed to something more top forties. I closed my eyes and let go, dancing my worries away, my fear wiped clean.

I danced like there was no tomorrow. Camille and I swung Corrine between us and laughed the entire time. We were joined by Catherine, Kendall, and even Maria Rosa, and Mrs. Clynes did some booty-shaking on the dance floor with us. Every now and then, I'd glance in Naseem's direction. Though he would smile when our eyes met, there was something wrong. I felt it in my marrow. Because that smile didn't reach his eyes.

Rahim joined us on the dance floor, and when the slow song played, he took Camille into his arms, and I kind of wished Naseem would have done the same to me.

~

HAD SHE REALLY JUST SAID SHE WANTED CHILDREN—plural—with me? I wanted to kick myself for not telling her I had no intention of bringing children into this world and she would just have to deal with it. The thought made me sick to my stomach. Out of nowhere, an image of two kids, a boy and a girl the age of Corinne and Chris but with olive skin and dark eyes, appeared. The little girl had dark, long wavy hair like Summer and the same beauty mark on the apple of her cheek. The vision was both beautiful and heartbreaking at the same time.

Mostly because that part of the story would never be. I won't have children just to abandon them. I wouldn't chance leaving my children wanting for parents, stability, or a home. Since I couldn't guarantee that I would live past forty, I couldn't accept the idea of having children. Nope. Not going to happen. *Ever*.

The celebrations moved on with a lot more food and alcoholic beverages than should probably be consumed in one sitting, but it was nice to sit and watch everyone have a great time.

Summer spent most of the afternoon dancing around with Corinne, and that just made me feel worse. I had to tell her about me not wanting kids, but I was worried she'd flee the instant I did.

"Let's go for a walk." I wrapped my arms around her waist the moment I found her freed up.

"Okay."

Her warm hand found mine, and that feeling of fullness was a little overpowering. My chest clenched with fear. The sun had started to set, and the sweet and salty night air was welcoming, but the sound of the crashing waves mirrored my insides—wild and thrashing. We walked in silence for a while, both lost within our own minds.

"I still have to break the news to my mom and Laith. I think he needs a phone call and an explanation."

"What are you going to tell them?"

"A censored truth about this week."

"Censored?"

"Yeah, neither of them needs to hear all about the earth-shattering sex we've been having or about us getting naughty in the waterfall." She laughed.

"We got naughty in the waterfall, huh? What was so naughty?" I stopped us from walking and pulled her body flush against mine.

"I think watching you masturbate while I fingered myself could be considered naughty." Her voice took on that smoky undertone that made my dick hard with just one word, and she pressed herself against my arousal.

"I want to get naughty again, but I'm not sure you have the balls for it," I teased.

Her fingers traveled down my length and I stifled a groan. This woman's wicked hands could play me like a music box made just for her amusement.

"I think I'm up for any challenge you have for me."

"Will you let me eat your pussy right here in the sand, where anyone could come by, anyone could watch?"

"How?"

"I want you on me riding my face."

She took my hand and placed it between her slick folds. "I'm ready for you."

"No underwear?"

"Nope. Didn't have a seamless pair to wear with this dress."

I took her lips with mine and kissed her while taking us down to the sand. Her greedy hands were in my hair and beneath the hem of my shirt within seconds. I lay back, and she sat on my chest.

"No, sweet pea. Give me that honey."

She stood and looked around carefully before lifting her already short dress and sitting back down on my face. She tasted like peaches, cream, and honey, and I devoured her. She wasn't quiet either, riding my face like she was at a rodeo.

When she finally let go, she orgasmed with my name on her lips, and my heart swelled with pride.

"You're really good at that." She slid down my body and caressed me through my pants. "It's my turn."

She unzipped my khakis and my cock saluted her. She licked the head and then took all of me. But I wanted something else. I wanted inside of her. I couldn't shake the feeling that somehow I'd fucked up and this might be our last time.

I stopped her and she looked at me, confused. "No?"

"I want inside that pussy." I handed her a condom. "Put this on and get on top of me." She did as I'd instructed, and fuck me, it was fucking awesome. First, she looked around again to make sure no one was watching, and then, like a naughty girl, she took my cock in her hand and directed me into her tight, wet heat.

It was hot, passionate kisses, radical movements, moans of passion, hair pulling, the most out-of-control lovemaking I'd ever had. Because it *was* lovemaking. I couldn't love her any more than I did at this very moment. This woman was my world. My whole fucking world.

"I love you." I whispered the words against her lips, and she moaned into my mouth. "I love you." I trailed kisses down her neck, behind her ears, and her movements became clumsy. Her body shuddered, and we climaxed together. She laid her head on my shoulder, and her body trembled with sobs. My heart sank.

"Hey." I pushed her hair from her face and attempted to have her look at me, but it wasn't any use. "What's going on? Talk to me."

"Don't break my heart again."

"I don't intend to."

She lifted her face to stare into my eyes. I knew that look. She had questions, but fear also danced behind her brown orbs.

"Well, Carter's mom said you never wanted kids, and when I mentioned wanting two just like Chris and Corinne, you ignored my statement. And that scared the crap out of me."

My heart was beating a mile a minute in my chest. How was I going to explain this to her without losing her?

"Because, you know, kids are important to me. I want

to have a legacy to leave behind—a handsome boy like you, and a sweet little girl that's a mini-me."

"Why, because it's on your ten-year plan?"

It was like I'd slapped her with words.

"No, it's because I love kids and I want a family. I thought you wanted one too, a family with me."

She pushed off of me but I pulled her back down. "You can't just walk away."

"You can't just ask me to marry you and then lay something like this on me. We used to talk about having kids and our own family unit in high school. Now that you're a grown-ass man, that isn't appealing to you?"

"I was an inexperienced kid. I had no concept of life and loss. I saw the world through rose-colored glasses. I'm not that guy anymore."

"What's that supposed to mean?"

I sighed and covered my face with both hands. Her scent all over my face and hands gave me the courage to divulge my fears. Because right now, I was scared of losing her more than sounding like a punk.

"I'm going to die before I turn forty."

"What?" The look of anger was replaced with a complete "what the fuck are you talking about" expression.

"Both my parents died of natural causes before their fortieth birthday."

"Just because your parents died young doesn't mean you will also die young."

"How do you know that I won't?"

"That's ridiculous, Naseem. You can't know when you're going to die. No one knows that, and you are a healthy young man. The odds of you dying before forty of natural causes are really slim. You have a greater chance of getting struck by lightning."

"What about my parents?"

"Honey, it was just their time."

"Why them? Huh? Why did my brother and I have to lose both parents when we were barely out of high school?"

"I don't know." Her warm hand caressed my cheek.

"Well, that's why I don't want kids. I don't want to have kids and leave them without a dad. I can't have children and just abandon them for their mother to raise on her own. It's not fair to the kids."

"Are you saying you won't have children with me, even though you asked me to marry you less than twenty-four hours ago?"

"I'm sorry."

She stared down at me for a long time. "I'm sorry too."

I tried to stop her, but she got to her feet. "Where are you going?"

"I need to think."

"Think about what? Me? Us?"

"Yes, all of it."

"Kids are more important to you than being together?"

"Not more important, but just as important. I want a family, Naseem. I was going to marry a stranger just so that I could have a family unit since I thought love wasn't in the cards. Now I have you back and you throw this at me?"

"What do you want me to say?"

"I want you to say that you love me and that you want a family with me."

I stood and towered over her. "You know I love you. I

didn't have to tell you. I could have said nothing and just gotten a vasectomy. You wouldn't have known about it until it was too late."

She recoiled. "That would have been despicable. I can't believe you could even think it, much less say it."

I covered my face. "I know, I'm sorry. I don't know why I said that."

"I do. You want to do everything you can to push me away, just like you did when you broke up with me the last time."

"What? No. What are you talking about?"

"It was just like last time, telling me those hateful things. Well, don't worry, Naseem Kakos, I got your message, loud and clear."

"What message? This wasn't something I planned. Can't you see it's killing me?"

"Right, sure. Whatever."

"Summer, look at me."

Her brown eyes burned into mine. "Fool me once, shame on you. Fool me twice, I'm a fucking idiot."

"You are overreacting." When she who used food words for curse words started saying swear words, I knew I was in trouble, but I didn't think I could stop this train wreck now, even if I tried.

"Overreacting? Me, overreacting? You just spend four days fucking me, you asked me to marry you, and I nearly broke off my arranged marriage, almost told my parents about you, then you pull this shit? Yeah, I'm overreacting."

"It wasn't like you didn't like the fucking, Summer. You liked it just fine when you were riding my face and dick."

"You are despicable."

"And you liked every bit of my dirty mouth."

"Yes, I did. You fucked me good. But you know, so does my favorite vibrator."

This time, she walked away, and I let her go, then fell to the sand, my legs lead, my heart pounding and chest constricting. Nausea rolled through me. What the hell just happened?

CHAPTER 13

Stupid. Stupid. Stupid. I let him do it to me again. I let him play me, lie to me, and then toss me away like garbage. I hurried back to the villa, my tears pouring down my face so hard I could barely see my way back. But it was the music that helped guide my way.

Finally, I made it but then slowed my step. I couldn't let anyone see the hot mess I was right now. I wiped away my tears and searched for the least exposed way to get inside without being noticed. Finally, without any other option, I decided to circle around and use the front door. I prayed it wasn't locked.

Thank God, the door was open, and I snuck in, but I should've known it wasn't going to be that easy. Camille and Catherine were both coming out of the kids' room, giggling about the monkey sleeping beside Christopher when they spotted me.

"Cleaning up after a quickie on the beach?" Camille teased.

"I hate when I get sand in my undies." Catherine giggled.

I froze at the sound of their voices. I didn't want to admit what a fool I'd been and just wanted to wash him off of me, get in my pajamas, and go to sleep.

"Yeah." I kept my head down and my back to them.

"What's wrong?" Camille's spy intuition kicked in, and I was screwed.

"Nothing, I, umm... I think I'm just going to call it a night. You okay with me still sleeping in here?" I kept walking to our room and opened the door.

"Of course you can. Did you and Naseem have a fight?"

"Yes, and please, I don't want to talk about it."

Camille nodded and backed out of the room to where Catherine was waiting quietly.

"Let us know if you need anything?" Catherine said. "I'll keep my phone on me. You don't have to come out of the room if you don't want to see anyone. Just text me."

"Thanks."

I hated the desperation in my voice. I thought I'd gotten rid of this weak version of me. I was strong now, tougher now. I was a fucking fighter. I'd lived through our first break-up, and I would be damned if this little fuck fest was going to be the reason I went back to being that pathetic girl again. I mean, since I'd laid eyes on Naseem, I'd said the F-word like ten times, and I didn't even curse.

I stripped out of my clothes and stared at my reflection. Weak. My eyes were bloodshot, my nose was red, and mascara-colored tears streamed down my face like I was a rookie peeling and chopping onions. I swatted away my tears and rubbed my eyes with firm swipes of my thumb and forefinger.

I was left with raccoon circles underneath my eyes,

but the frustration of seeing my horrible reflection only seemed to fuel a new set of tears.

I turned on the tub water to nearly scalding and didn't wait for it to fill to the rim before stepping inside. Right now, I really wished I had a shower, but a bath would have to do. The water worked to heat my muscles, and I curled into a ball in the center of the bathtub, my body trembling with scorching tears. I allowed myself that one last cry. Then, I'd be done. I wasn't going to ever cry over him or any man again. I was absolutely, positively, completely done.

I was right to go ahead with that arranged marriage proposal. Laith wasn't going to break my heart because he would never have my heart. That shredded piece of me belonged to only one man, and he couldn't seem to keep from breaking it.

I stayed in the tub until the water was cool, my tears had dried, and my heart was firmly duct-taped back together. Then, I dressed in the most comfortable pair of pajamas I had with me, took a sleeping pill, and crashed. I didn't want to think or feel any more tonight. I just needed a whole lot of REM sleep. When morning came, I'd pack my shit and act like this little detour never happened. I was going to get on that plane to marry a man that would never have the power to break my heart, because you can't break something already broken.

~

Holy hell. Did I fall asleep in the bathtub or something? But no, waves washed over my legs, and the sound of the ocean was just too damn close. Was that sand beneath me? I attempted to open my eyes, but the sun was just too bright. What happened? The last thing I remembered was the fight with Summer and grabbing a bottle of Johnny Walker Blue. Rubbing my eyes with the back of my hand, I seemed to do more damage than good when grains of sand stung my eyes. I took the inside of my shirt and wiped. Finally, my vision returned, but for the life of me, I couldn't remember how I'd landed back in the same spot where Summer and I had fought.

Oh, Summer. What had I done yesterday? The things I said. They'd seemed rational then. It was the perfect way out of the mess I'd put us in. I couldn't be with her only halfway. I couldn't be one foot in and one foot out of this relationship. It was either all in or all out. And last night, while faced with my fears, I'd chosen to punk out. I'd taken the easy way out, and I felt like shit. I'd promised her I wouldn't hurt her again, but I did. Fuck.

The least I could do was say sorry for the way I'd acted and come clean. Tell her that I loved her, but I just couldn't ever be a father, and if she walked away then, it would be her choice.

I made it back to the villa where Camille was sitting on the patio with a cup of coffee and watching the kids play in the nearby sandbox.

"Hey." I braced myself for an attack, because if looks could kill, I'd be full of holes and bleeding right now.

"You know, I'm getting sick and tired of you playing games with my friend's heart."

"This has nothing to do with you."

"Nothing to do with me. Seriously? Are you"—she glanced in the kids' direction and then back at me —"fucking kidding me? I was the one who found her after you broke her heart at the back door of the school. I was the one who watched out for her all summer long after you discarded her like yesterday's trash, and today, I was the one who helped her pack her shit so that she would get as far away from you as fucking possible."

"What? Where is she?"

"I'm not telling you. But she gave me this to give to you." She pulled out a little envelope and handed it to me, then she turned away and joined the kids in the sandbox.

My hands trembled when I opened the envelope and saw it was a picture. A picture of us from high school. It was, in fact, the same picture she used to keep in her planner on her first vision board. When I'd asked about the picture, she'd said she'd burned it, but she hadn't. She actually had been carrying it around with her. My legs gave out, and I fell into the chair Camille had been sitting on.

I stared at the image of young us, dressed for prom. She'd looked like a sexy mermaid in a stunning fitted gold-beaded dress that hugged her body, and I looked like a skinny punk, but I'd thought I was so cool to be wearing my tuxedo and taking the most beautiful girl at the school to prom.

What happened to us, Summer? Where did those two bright-eyed teens go? This picture was taken only a few days before I'd heard about my father's cancer.

I felt a warm hand on my shoulder. "Don't cry, Nas." I looked up, and tiny Corrine was standing in front of me. She patted my cheek. "Everything is going to be okay. All you have to do is say you're sorry, and Summer will forgive you."

She climbed onto my lap and her little arms went around my neck, and the little shred of resistance I had crumbled. She was just like her mother, in spirit and looks. Just like Camille was like Mrs. Clynes.

Then it all hit me like a ton of bricks. That image of the boy was a young me, and I was the spitting image of my dad. If I didn't leave a piece of me behind, even if I died young, a piece of my parents would be gone too. Unless Nash had kids, my parents' legacy would be gone forever. I realized I didn't want to die. I realized I couldn't live like I was going to die. And for the first time in my life, I realized how precious children were and how life with them was only more enriched. That vision of the boy and girl that looked like a mixture of me and Summer came back to me, and everything inside me screamed at my stupidity.

Camille placed a gentle hand on my shoulder. "She got on the plane to Argentina. If you are going to man up and stop with your crazy games, go stop her from making the biggest mistake of her life. Go get our girl."

"I can't. What about you guys? You're supposed to be going home tomorrow."

"What's a couple more days in *Jenna* going to hurt?"

"*Jenna*?" I asked, half laughing, half crying.

"Yes, Heaven. Rahim has been teaching me a little bit of Arabic."

"Really?"

"Yup, he calls me *mish mish*."

"Peach?"

"What can I say? He says I remind him of peaches." She giggled.

I kissed Corrine on the cheek and set her on the ground. "Thank you, sweetheart. You really made me feel better."

"You're welcome. Go get our girl, like Mama said."

She smiled, and it made my heart melt. "Yes, ma'am."

I turned to Camille and kissed her cheek as well.

"Thanks for always being there for my girl, even when I was too stupid to be myself."

I checked my pockets, looking for my phone, to no avail. Where the hell was it? I was rushing inside when Rahim was coming out to the patio with a cup of coffee. I took Rahim's cup out of his hand. It was full up, and odds were he hadn't even had a sip yet.

"Just how you like it, black like your soul." Rahim rolled his eyes. "Where the hell were you?"

"Passed out on the beach, apparently, with a bottle of Johnny Walker."

"Red or Black label?"

"Does it matter?"

"Yes, I'm trying to get a clear picture of how pathetic you looked."

"Stop acting like a dick and help me find my phone."

"I have your phone. You left it on the table last night."

"Good, call the airport and tell them I'm taking off in an hour. I have to shower really quickly and then I'm going."

"Not without me," Rahim said.

"It's not necessary."

"I think it might be."

"Whatever. Be ready in ten."

I almost made my way to my room, but not before I was stopped by Carter's voice. "'Not a Second Time.'"

"I'm in no mood for your Beatles sarcasm."

"Fine, here's something genuine from me. Don't fuck it up twice."

"I know." I covered my face. "I fucked up, really bad, and Camille just let me have it. I'm going to get her. Will you check on Rahim while he's scheduling us for takeoff? Will you guys be good until I get back?"

"Yeah, Maria Rosa has this place held for us for the rest of the week."

"Cool." I took in a jagged breath. "What if she doesn't forgive me?"

"Well, you have to be convincing."

"How?"

"'Revolution'?" He used another one of the Beatles song titles. "Seriously though, at least you tried. Could you live with yourself if you didn't?"

"No."

He patted me on the shoulder, and I finally made it into my room for a shower. After brushing my teeth and a quick wash of the important parts, I was dressed and ready to go in ten minutes.

Rahim was waiting for me on the patio. "The cab will take too long, so Carter's driving us in Maria Rosa's Jeep."

"Let's roll."

We made it to the airport in record time, and before we knew it, we were on our way to Argentina. And hopefully, to use the last Beatles song title Carter threw at me just before he left, "'All We Need is Love.'"

~

IT WAS LIKE I WAS SUFFERING FROM A SERIOUS CASE of what-the-fucks while I waited at the airport for my flight to take off. My phone beeped, and I thought it was Camille checking on me, but it was my mom on Skype.

After the hotel with he-who-must-not-be-named, I'd forgotten my phone in my fanny pack and let the thing die until this morning when I'd finally charged it and found five voicemails from my mother. If I didn't answer now, she was going to contact the CIA and report me missing and a possible human trafficking victim.

"Hi, Mama." I did my best to smile, but I was sure she'd see right through it.

"Hi, *bentie*. Where have you been?" Her calling me "my daughter" in Arabic broke whatever resolve I'd had, and the tears just started to roll. I wasn't supposed to cry. I'd sworn last night in the tub was the last time. But you know what? Sometimes, a girl just needed to be comforted by her mama.

So I told her about Naseem being there, about how we'd reconnected, leaving out being lost in the forest and the sex, but I told her about his proposal and our breakup. I told her about his fears of death, and when I was finally finished, I'd stopped crying, but my mother had started.

"Oh, *habibi*, I wish I was there. I would chase him with my shoe for hurting my baby girl again."

The image of my four-foot-eleven mother chasing Naseem with her house shoe brought on the giggles. She laughed too. "What are you going to do now? Coming home? What about Laith?"

"He doesn't know any of this yet. Actually, I"—I hesitated—"I know you and Baba want me to marry him because of the deal in Jordan."

"That has nothing to do with that. It was an added bonus because we would be family, but the agreement was in the works before your proposal. How in the world would you think your father and I would, what, sell you?"

Her word hit me hard in the back of the head. How in the world could I believe that my parents would be that heartless?

"Besides, your sister is married to his cousin, so we already had an in without you." She laughed.

"I feel like a fool."

"Look at me, *bentie*."

I made eye contact with my mom over the camera, and the love I've always known was there shined back at me. How could I possibly believe they only cared for me out of dignity and traditional values?

"Marry Laith, don't marry Laith, Marry Nas..."

"Don't say his name."

"Sorry, *bentie*, sorry. Marry the idiot, or not—either way, it's your life. We just want you happy."

"I think I want what you and Baba have. A marriage built on trust, respect, and mutual interest."

"But we are also in love, even though I want to hit him with my house shoes half the time."

"You said love came later."

"It did, but neither of us loved someone else."

"So are you saying I should just forget it and come home?"

"I'm saying you should be following your heart."

"I don't trust my heart right now."

"Well, make a list. You're good at these things. Pros, cons. And let that help you make the answer."

I laughed. My mom always knew me best. I wished I could hug her and just get one whiff of her comforting scent of Coco Chanel, but she was thousands of miles away.

"When does your flight leave?"

"In forty-five minutes." Panic burned in my chest.

"Well, take out some paper. I know you have it with your planner. Make that list. Do you want me to stay on the phone?"

"No. I think I have to do that on my own."

"Okay, *habibi*. You make that list, and let me know what you decide."

"Mom, thank you."

"Just doing my job as your mother. No matter how old you get, you will always be my child."

Tears pricked my eyes. After we said our goodbyes, I sat down with a tall drink at the bar, pulled out my planner, and made a list of the pros and cons of marrying Laith. I had to say, there would be many pros—first and foremost, a marriage built on trust, respect, and mutual goals like my parents'. He wanted a family—actually, two kids. He'd mentioned that in one of our short and awkward conversations. Awkward conversations, now that was a negative. I didn't love him, didn't think I could ever fall in love with him if I was in love with someone else. We didn't really have anything in common.

I was a reader, loved fantasy and paranormal. He'd once said he thought reading fiction was a waste of time. That was definitely a con.

I wrote all the things I could think of, from physical attraction to taste in food and drinks. Not to mention the fact that I'd actually have to have sex with him. Would I be able to do that? Out of all these things on the list, getting intimate with Laith scared the hell out of me. Before reconnecting with Naseem, I didn't think much of it, but now, sharing my body with anyone else was just something I couldn't wrap my head around. But I kept coming back to one thing—children. I wanted to be a mom. I wanted to have that relationship with my daughter that I had with my mother. I wanted a piece of me to live on in someone else. The image of Naseem playing airplanes with little Chris that first morning had zapped me in the heart, and I hadn't been able to breathe.

"Flight 505 to Buenos Aires is now boarding." The intercom blared through the airport. My time was up. I had to decide now. Marry a stranger, or head back home with my tail between my legs. I downed the rest of my drink and looked down at my notes. One column was slightly longer than the other. I guessed that was my answer. Before gathering my things, I texted my mom letting her know my decision and prayed I was doing the right thing.

THE LANDING IN BUENOS AIRES WAS PROBABLY THE most out-of-control landing of my entire flying career. My body vibrated with nervous tension. My throat was dry, and my hands even tingled. I was sweaty and nausea rolled through me.

"You okay?" Rahim sat beside me in the copilot seat ready to take over if I passed out, but luckily, I was able to get us grounded before heading to the bathroom and vomiting. Fucking Johnny Walker.

After I'd brushed with the spare toothbrush I kept on the plane for really long flights, my chest tightened and my pulse raced. *Will she forgive me?*

It was a matter of minutes to get through air control and customs, or was it hours? I couldn't remember—it was all I could do to stay upright. Finally, we were walking through the airport, and I was frantically looking around for her. I flinched when I saw any girl with waist-length chocolate brown hair. But none of them were Summer. None of them were my girl.

While I wallowed in my misery, I followed Rahim around the airport. And now I understood why he'd insisted on coming with me. I really needed the support at this moment, and thank God Rahim was such a nag. We made it outside, and the fresh air kissed my face. I breathed in the sunlight, and the sound of a laugh halted me. It was her laugh. Her awkward, I-feel-weird laugh, but it was hers.

First, I believed I was hearing things, but Rahim tapped me on the arm and pointed to a girl a few steps away. Wild curly hair blew in the breeze, and her yellow sundress shimmered against her skin like sunshine. Her back was to us, and I froze, not sure what to do next.

"It's now or never, bro. They're in the cab line."

"Right."

Camille's voice from this morning echoed in my mind's eye. *"Man up."* I wasn't sure if those were her exact words, but I was pretty sure that was what she'd say if she were here beside me.

I made my way over to where she stood. Her back was still to me. This would have been better if I'd gone the other way so we'd make eye contact. But I couldn't get my legs to move any farther.

Then I realized she was standing with someone. He was just about her height since, even with her heels, she was just barely five-foot-three inches tall. He looked the same—clean-shaven, still skinny, but a little broader than his eighteen-year-old self. He placed a hand on her arm, and I think I growled. Laith's eyes found mine, and he recoiled. Everything I'd been feeling, the illness, the uneasiness, was gone the moment he touched my girl. Instead, rage and jealousy took over, and my balls that I'd momentarily lost returned.

"Summer."

Her spine immediately stiffened. Even though her back was to me, I could tell her eyes were closed, and she counted to five. I counted along, and on five, she turned to face me.

CHAPTER 14

This seriously couldn't be happening. Naseem Fucking Kakos was not standing in front of me right fucking now. Fuck. Fuck. Fuck. I was using the F-word again. Goddamn it. Even though I wanted to knee him in the balls for following me all the way here, my heart and lady parts celebrated at the sight of him. They were traitors, the both of them. My head was the only one with any common sense at the moment, and it was screaming all kinds of obscenities at me to remember the hot mess I'd been in just last night. The memory of my mascara-tear-streamed face and the gut-wrenching pain his words caused were the exact reminder I needed at this moment.

"What are you doing here?" My ice-cold tone was strange to my own ears. Every syllable, I uttered with thoughtful intention to stay as indifferent as possible.

"Can we talk?"

"Say what you have to say and go."

"Alone." He pointed over my shoulder, and I glanced behind me. Laith watched quietly. I read the "what the fuck" in his expression, and guilt washed over me. I'd been so unfair to him.

I sighed. "I'm so sorry. Can you give us a minute?"

Laith nodded, and I let Naseem lead me a few paces away. He attempted to put his hand on the small of my back, but I recoiled. My heart hammered in my chest, and my legs felt as though they were encased in blocks of cement.

"Do not touch me," I warned.

"I'm sorry." He lifted both hands in the air in surrender. We made it to a smoker's corner, and he finally turned to face me. It was the first time I noticed his dark circles and red-rimmed eyes. His normally olive skin's sun-kissed hue had a grey undertone. My traitorous heart tugged.

"What do you want?"

"I'm sorry." He attempted to hold my hands, and I backed away. "Shit, fuck. I'm sorry." He ran his fingers through his unkempt locks of hair the way I longed to. "I love you. I can't live without you. Please forgive me."

It was as though someone threw ice-cold water in my face. "Now, you have these words. Where were they last night? When you were too busy saying all those nasty and hurtful things."

"Okay, you're right. I'm scared. I'm scared of marriage, of having children, but most importantly, I'm terrified that I'll die young and leave you as a widow with children to care for all on your own. I am terrified that my kids will lose their dad way too early like I did. I was only eighteen, and I was completely lost. I felt homeless despite the countless family members that tried to make Nash and I feel welcome. Losing my parents was like losing part of myself."

My already tattered heart was bleeding for him, but I'd learned all this last night, and I had to protect myself from breaking down in front of him.

"I'm sorry you went through everything you did. No matter how old you are, losing parents so close and so young is not easy. But what does all this have to do with the hateful things you said yesterday?"

"I was afraid. Like I was all those years ago, and I punked out. It took you leaving, the picture, and little Corinne to make me realize I was doing a dishonor to my parents' memory by not having children. Not helping to continue their legacy."

My heart hammered. It was everything I'd sought to hear last night and the last thing I needed right now. He now wanted children. Now? Was he fucking kidding me? There I went with the F-words again. He appeared, and all of a sudden, I was Tony Montana. White-hot fury washed over me.

"Good for you. Go. I'm sure there are many women willing to be your baby mama, but I'm not one of them. I'm done with your lies, I'm done with your games, and most importantly, I'm done with you."

"Summer, please."

"If you don't have anything else to say, my fiancé is over there waiting."

"I thought you loved me?" he whispered.

"I've loved you my whole life and will always love you, but I can't trust you won't hurt me again. And my heart can't take another disappointment." My voice splintered my words.

"Please." His dark stare burned into mine.

I grasped his trembling hand between my own and squeezed. "It's for the best. I think we both have the power to hurt each other very deeply. It's not healthy. We aren't good for each other."

He hung his head, and it took everything in me not to cave and collapse into his arms. He lifted our joined hands and pressed his lips to my palm. A warm, single tear touched my fingertip.

"Take care of yourself," I whispered. With shaky and unsteady legs, I walked back to the cabstand where Laith was not-so-patiently waiting.

I glanced behind me, but Naseem was gone. Panic ripped through me. I looked around, my heart beating out of control. Then I caught him and Rahim going back inside the airport.

"What is going on?" Laith's confused and wary voice made me get my shit together and get back to the situation at hand. The poor guy looked so perplexed. I was supposed to be visiting as his blushing bride-to-be, but instead, I'd shown up broken, tattered, and trailed by my ex-boyfriend.

"I'm so sorry. For everything." My apology was for more than what just happened, and he was smart enough to catch on.

"Was that Naseem?"

"Yeah."

"He looks different. But I thought you and he weren't together anymore."

"I...I don't know where to begin. Can we sit down somewhere? We really need to talk."

He pointed at a bench a few feet away and I nodded my head. With legs that felt like cooked noodles, I followed him to the bench he directed us to. I told him an abbreviated version of the past few days, leaving out the sex parts, and explained how Naseem and I had reconnected. But I also explained that we couldn't be together because we weren't good for each other.

"Wow. That's a lot, yes."

I examined Laith's features. He was a handsome man with big hazel eyes, dark brown, straight hair that he wore slicked back off his face, and tanned skin. He was muscular and well dressed. But all I could see were Naseem's downcast eyes and his trembling lips when they'd touched my palm.

"I'm sorry, but...I can't marry you. I feel like suck a jerk. You deserve so much better than this mess. My heart is broken, and I don't know if it will ever heal. You don't deserve that. You deserve a girl to love you just the way you deserve to be loved."

"Before he came, you were going to marry me even after all that happened?"

Guilt washed over me. "Yes. That was wrong. I was marrying you for the wrong reasons. And you deserve better."

"If you didn't have plane trouble, you would have married me."

"Yes, but I guess it was serendipity." The words were out before I knew it, and my heart hemorrhaged at the memory of Naseem calling our chance encounter that day like the movie *Serendipity*. Did I make the wrong decision? Should I have accepted his apology and gotten on that plane with him? His disheveled appearance, the sorrow in his expression, the sadness in his eyes had nearly killed me. That look on his face would forever haunt me.

"Serendipity? Chance, yes?"

His confused voice brought me back to the moment—

the current cluster that my bad choices had brought me to.

"I think someone up there was looking out for us both by adding this divergence." I pointed up to the heavens. "There is something else planned for the both of us." As I spoke the words, they resonated with me. Maybe it was Naseem's parents or my grams, or maybe both, plotting to get us together.

"I always cared for you. The honest truth... I was surprised you accepted. But such is life."

Well, he really didn't seem thrown by our breakup. I think I was more hurt by it than he. Well, that was good—less burden on my already tattered heart.

"What would you like to do, get another plane?"

"Actually, I have a hotel reservation. I think I need a long, hard sleep before I get on another plane."

"We are still friends, yes?"

"Always." I gave him a small smile.

"Yes, let me buy you lunch and escort you to the hotel safety. This will make me feel better. My parents will kill me if I do not."

"Okay."

UNFORTUNATELY, I DON'T REMEMBER HOW WE MADE it back to the villa. I flew—with Rahim right beside me—but after we'd landed, I'd completely shut down. I only remember taking the nearest bottle and heading to my room in the villa. I don't think anyone bothered me. That first night, I'd already been sick from the binge from the night before, and after a few deep drags of this next bottle, I passed out until I felt someone nagging me awake.

"What?" I groaned. My eyes hurt too much to do anything more than squint.

"You need to eat something." Carter was using his take-no-bullshit tone.

"It's still morning. I never eat breakfast."

"You've been sleeping for forty-eight hours."

"How?" I sounded like I'd smoked a carton of cigarettes. My throat dry and scratchy, I nearly coughed out a lung. I looked around for a glass of water or even the liquor bottle I'd been drinking from, but instead, a cup of black coffee was shoved in my face.

"Drink this. There is also is a bottle of water and Tylenol on the dresser."

"Bring them here." I groaned again.

"Nope, your ass will have to get out of bed to get them. And I'm suggesting you take a shower and have something to eat after you do."

"I don't think I can." It sounded even more pathetic out loud. How did I get here? Summer. Her face appeared to me like an apparition. Beautiful smile, bright dark eyes, and a mane of hair that I adored wrapping around my fingertips. It wasn't the Summer from just a few days ago, it was the Summer in that picture of us as children, still clutched in my hand even in my sleep. The image in my mind's eye transformed into a different Summer. This one was the girl I'd left at the airport. Mistrust and heartbreak replaced the pure joy that had been there.

I'd put that expression there. I took a gorgeous soul and reduced it to a hollow shell of what she once was—a soul filled with love, passion, and courage. A soul filled with a yearning for life and the adventures that sprang from the experiences.

"Listen. I'm only going to say this once. It's your choice if you're interested. This is the number to the counselor I was seeing to deal with all the Lucy stuff. It was cool to be able to talk and just get things off my chest."

I started to argue, but then I remembered how Carter still had unresolved feelings about Lucy's death up until a while ago. Lucy was Carter's high school girlfriend who committed suicide after they broke up and Carter went away to college. He'd always blamed himself for not realizing Lucy needed help.

I nodded. I wasn't going to knock the process that had worked for him. What's the saying, the proof is in the pudding? Carter was now in a healthy place mentally and was married to the love of his life. While the only girl who ever meant anything to me was probably already married to someone else. Probably sharing his bed. Bile burned my throat, and Carter got his wish. I was out of bed and kneeling in front of the toilet, retching the few sips of coffee I'd just drunk.

While I washed my face and brushed my teeth, Carter had followed me into the bathroom, turned on the tub for a bath, and gone out the door.

"If you don't come out of this room in half an hour, I will send Camille, and I'm pretty sure you wouldn't want to deal with all of that attitude right now."

"Fine. Just go."

I'd been sleeping for forty-eight hours. How could that be possible? Then I remembered, every time I'd attempted to get up, I'd recalled what happened and didn't have the energy to get out of bed. Eventually, I'd fallen back asleep.

If there was one thing I knew, I couldn't live like this,

and I couldn't continue living my life the way it was—no roots anywhere, flying all over the world, damn near living out of my suitcase, and sleeping with a different woman every night. I owed it to my parents to actually live and not just pretend to live in this hollow existence I'd created for myself.

I soaked in the tub until the water was cold and Camille knocked on my bedroom door. But when I stepped out of this room, I was going to mend my ways. I was going to be a better man, and I was going to find the strength to deal with my fears of my mortality and, possibly one day, be able to live up to my father's legacy.

"Naseem Kakos, you've got five minutes to come out or I'm coming in," Camille threatened from outside the door. The seriousness in her voice made me chuckle. My chest was a little lighter. I was still grieving, heartbroken and disappointed in the way things had turned out, but somehow, I was putting my big boy pants on and had made a plan. That's something Summer would do, and maybe making plans, having goals, would help me be close to my girl, even if she wasn't with me.

CHAPTER 15

It was my second full week home in Michigan in like forever. Since I'd canceled my wedding and honeymoon, I didn't have any travel work plans on the docket for another month, at least. I was still working, which I desperately needed to keep me busy, and there were always emails to answer, sales calls to take, and mandatory meetings to attend in the Michigan office. But it was the late nights when I struggled with turning off my brain and sleeping. Every time I closed my eyes, I saw Naseem's face. Sometimes it was that erotic sexy smile, and other times, it was the brokenhearted expression from that day at the airport. I was still plagued with the guilt of my actions. With both Laith and Naseem.

That was when I started night-baking everything from cheesecakes to baklava. Other times, I'd roll pots of dolmas for each of my siblings. Last night, I'd baked a ridiculous amount of meat-and-cheese pies for my dad's breakfast and delivered a batch to each of my siblings on my way to work.

Anything to keep my mind engaged. Anything to stop

myself from obsessing about what could have been if I hadn't let him walk away. Would he have changed his mind or gotten cold feet? Would he have freaked out again and pushed me away? Or had he really changed because of me? Would we be planning our wedding and looking for a house together?

These questions still overwhelmed me when I missed the U-turn on Telegraph Road toward my sister Sara's house, and I found myself right in front of the old, white three-story Victorian building from my original vision board from high school—the one I'd dreamed would become my future restaurant. I pulled into the parking lot, which was more like an elegant circle driveway, that led into a larger parking area in the back. I eased my car in front of the building and stared at the FOR SALE sign.

My pulse rushed to my ears, and my heart hammered. I picked up my cell phone and dialed the number below the sign before I changed my mind. When the woman answered the phone, I almost hung up, but I found the courage to make the appointment to see the inside. The owner, Tamara, agreed to show me the space in ten minutes because, lucky for me, her office was just down the street. She might have heard the apprehension in my voice over the phone and decided she'd meet me herself since her agents were all busy today.

I called off of work for the first time in my entire adult career. Something was telling me I was doing the right thing. Maybe it was my dream realized, or maybe it was the adrenaline of doing something completely off my ten-year plan, but I was vibrating with excitement and fear.

It wasn't long before Tamara Jackson parked her slick black Mercedes next to me. The African American woman was about my age with long locks and New York-model fashion appeal. Her chic black tailored pantsuit was paired with red-bottomed shoes and chunky jewelry that gave her look the right pop of wow.

"Hey there, I'm Tamara."

"Hi, I'm Summer." I took her outreached hand and was comforted by her firm handshake and her warm smile. I turned my gaze back to my dream restaurant and stood paralyzed, taking it all in.

"Ready?" Tamara said.

Was I ready? Could I do this? Could I take this leap of faith and, for once, follow my dreams without putting them on some grand plan?

"Yes."

I followed her up the front steps of the building, already thinking of the ADA requirement for people in wheelchairs.

"There is an entrance with a ramp on the side of the building."

"I was just wondering about that."

"Great minds." She smiled.

"Holy fritters, let's do this."

~

"So, tell me, Naseem, what do you want to talk about?" Dr. Lemmon asked.

I stared at the checkered pattern of the rug in her office and the little burn mark in the center of the carpet. Looked like Dr. Lemmon sneak-smoked like Summer.

Fuck...Summer.

I was haunted by thoughts of her, day in and day out, and I was about to lose my mind.

"Nothing." I sat there with my arms crossed over my

chest and my eyes glued to the floor. Who was I? I didn't even recognize myself anymore. I was brooding like a kid sent to the principal's office.

"What brought you here?"

"My partners insisted I see someone." Carter had called my brother Nash, and since we are a three-person board, I was outvoted and forced to come here.

"Why would they do that?"

"I can't sleep, I can't eat, and I can't work."

"How long has this been going on?"

"Two weeks, two hours, and"—I glanced at my watch —"forty-five minutes."

"That's pretty precise. When did your sleeping pattern change?"

"After the nightmares started."

"What kind of nightmares? Tell me about them."

"They are about a girl, Summer. I keep seeing her with this man, laughing, happy, pregnant. Kissing him, making love to him. It makes me sick."

"Who is Summer?"

"The one that got away."

"Did you end the relationship or did she?"

"I messed up."

"I see. What exactly did you do?"

"I...don't know."

"You really don't know?"

"Well, I apologized when I realized the error of my ways, but she picked him. She wasn't supposed to pick him. She was supposed to marry me."

"Tell me what happened. Why did she pick someone else?"

At first, having the conversation about my feelings, my nightmares, was weird, too fucking disturbing and mortifying, but once I started talking, it was like a dam broke, and I poured my heart out to this lady. It was such a relief to talk to someone who understood my mindset, who didn't judge me or condemn me because they knew I'd been the one to fuck everything up with Summer.

Needless to say, I made another appointment before I left for the day.

CHAPTER 16

Holy fritters. Happy big three-oh to me. Up until eight months ago, I had vast goals attached to my thirtieth birthday deadline with a laundry list of accomplishments I deemed were the only way to accurately measure success, but after returning home from Argentina, I realized what a true fool I'd been all those years. Lists, goals, and plans are important to have, but they can't be treated like the Holy Grail. Going off course from my ten-year plan freed me from the toxic relationship I had with myself. Now, I was able to explore the life I wanted instead of the life I presumed quantified my accomplishments. By letting go of the expectations I'd placed upon myself, I'd found passion and realized that, while climbing the corporate ladder was great for my savings account, it suppressed my appetite for life instead of nourishing it.

Floating on air, I held my arms out wide and circled the splendor of what used to be a shabby banquet hall. The space glimmered with mood lighting, each table decorated with lush bouquets of pink roses. The scents of herbs and spices infused the air. Everyone I loved and cared deeply for would be attending the grand opening of Sweet Pea—well, all but the one man I couldn't seem to forget.

After eight months, I still missed Naseem. How could four short days and nights still haunt me after two hundred and forty-two days? I'd filled my long days with work, and I was content, I was happy, but in the dead of the night, I was haunted by memories of his mischievous laugh, our heated banter, and our lovemaking. There was a large part of my heart that was empty and stony without him. I woke in cold sweats from the nightmares of our last fight and the defeated look in his eyes. It was a good thing I didn't have his number, or I would have broken down in the middle of the night and called him to profess my love. So many times, I'd wanted to kick myself for letting him walk away from me that day in the airport. It was in those quiet nights alone that I couldn't help but wonder if I had accepted his apology, would he be by my side? Would we be married already or planning our wedding? Or would he have gotten cold feet and jet set to God-knew-where?

Pushing my thoughts of him to the back of my mind, I admired my restaurant one last time before things kicked off. It took forever, but I'd finally renovated all three floors. The cathedral ceilings were lined with rustic wooden beams, and hanging crystal chandeliers sparkled from each plank, while crystal light pendants hung over each dining table and booth.

All the linens were crisp white, the silverware and glasses sparkled on each table, and the DJ for tonight's party was setting up. My team was getting the first course together, and I was supposed to be getting into my party dress, but I couldn't seem to walk away from the sweet table in the corner created by my new pastry chef.

The door chimed with the new bell I'd placed, and my heart did a dorky flip-flop at the adorable sound. A verse of the "Happy Birthday" song resonated from the door before I could even turn to greet my first arrivals. My heart beamed when Camille and little Corrine danced and sang into the dining room.

Camille stopped in her tracks on the way toward me. "Seriously, tell me you're changing into something else for tonight?"

She looked incredible, as always. A black fitted cocktail dress hugged her curves and fell to right above her knees. It had long sleeves and a plunging neckline with killer heels to match. I looked down at my leggings, stained white T-shirt, and Chucks, and did a small circle. "This isn't cute?"

"No, Summer. You look like Mama does when she's cleaning the house." Corrine giggled.

"Oh, someone thinks they're funny." I tickled her side. "Give me a spin so I can see how marvelous you look." Corrine blushed the cutest shade of pink and did an adorable spin for me that ended with a curtsy.

"You look every bit of the princess you are tonight." I turned to Corinne. "I do have a dress. It's actually a gift from Sara."

"I love her boutique. She has the most beautiful stuff."

"I hope so. I haven't even opened up the garment bag since she delivered it while I was in the kitchen getting ready for tonight."

"So I have something to tell you." Camille's expression stilled and my stomach sank.

"What?"

"Rahim is coming tonight as my date." The words spilled out of her mouth quickly, like if she said it fast enough, somehow, I wouldn't get angry. The thing was, I couldn't be angry with her.

"I didn't know you were still seeing him."

"It kind of just started happening. He was visiting his parents and called me last month."

"He comes over all the time. Sometimes, he comes over in the morning too. Before I'm even up for school," Corinne said.

I suppressed a giggle. "Before you wake up for school, huh? Wow, that is early, but I know your mama and Rahim are real early birds."

I glanced at Camille, and she was holding back a laugh too.

"I don't mind. I really like him, and he makes you happy. That's all that matters."

"Thank you." She hugged me tight. "Now go change before more people show up and you look like the night-shift cleaning crew instead of the birthday girl."

~

WHEN I WALKED INTO MY OFFICE, I WASN'T surprised to see Rahim and Carter whispering. That was the newest normal, and I'd bet my left nut they were being bitch-ass little girls gossiping about me. They kept trying to make me go out, but I had no desire to do anything. Even flying had lost its luster to me. One night, Carter had Kendall force me over for dinner, but it was an excuse to set me up with Kendall's friend. She was cute, and after a few drinks, she cornered me in the laundry room. But her hands on me caused physical pain, and my traitorous piece of shit dick wouldn't come to attention. It had failed me for the first time in my life.

But it wasn't broken when *it* woke me up with a hard-as-a-rock woody after a sex dream of Summer. I was ruined without Summer. It was my karma for what I'd done to her. I hurt her deeply twice, and this nightmare I was living in was the universe giving me what I deserved for my stupidity. She was with another man and probably pregnant with his child. And I was just here, neither living nor dying. Especially not today, because today was Summer's birthday, and she was probably celebrating it with her new husband in Argentina or wherever right now.

"We have something to tell you."

Here we went with another fucking lecture. Anger washed through me.

"Look, I'm not going to off myself, so no worries. Stop acting like gossiping hags and let me be."

"Summer isn't married. She never got married," Rahim spat.

My ears started ringing and I fell back into my chair. "What?"

"Bro, I just found out. Camille told me about it today. Apparently, she didn't get married. She quit her job and bought a restaurant."

"How? Why didn't anyone tell me?"

"'She's a Woman.'"

"Bro, enough with the Beatles titles. None of us were even born when those came out."

"Still good music."

"What restaurant?"

"That one off of Telegraph Road and Long Pine. The

white three-story building that looks like a house. I think it's been vacant for a while."

My pulse quickened in my ears. That was the place from her vision board—the original vision board from high school. I reached for my wallet and opened the front pocket. Our picture from prom was in the inside slot. Her beautiful bright smile warmed my broken heart.

Rahim held my overnight bag in his hand—I usually left one ready for emergency flights or important clients that called on short notice. "Bro, let's go."

"Where?" It didn't change the fact that I'd poured my heart out to her and she'd crushed it with the heel of her stiletto.

"It's her thirtieth birthday party and the grand opening of her new restaurant. Kendall and I are invited too." Carter placed the invitation on my desk, and I stared at it like it was a bomb that might just go off.

"That doesn't mean she wants me there." My fingers trembled around the card.

You are cordially invited to Summer Seba's 30th Birthday Party and the Grand Opening of Sweet Pea.

The card fell from my hand and onto the desk. "She named it Sweet Pea?"

"Wasn't that your nickname for her?" Carter asked.

"Yeah." My heart was beating a million miles a minute. Was that a hint for me? Or was I just over-thinking things?

"What if I go and she rejects me? I don't know if I'd survive that, not again." The truth was, I wasn't surviving without her, anyway. I was living in a cloud of sadness and loneliness.

Carter placed his hand on my shoulder. "At least you'll know. Either way, we got your back."

Blood rushed in my ears, and my body roared with excitement. "Let's go."

"Hey, Perky, let's go."

Kendall and her little baby bump peeked into the office. "Oh, goodie."

It wasn't long before we were all packed up and ready to fly to Michigan. The two-hour flight went by in a blur, and when Rahim tried to touch base with our Waterford Corporate Travel partners, they told us to stand by because of a mix-up with their flight schedule.

"They are saying to try Detroit Flight?" Rahim said.

"We don't have a car in that hangar. By the time we get a car, the party will be over."

"So, should I radio Detroit Flight or what?"

"Fuck. Yeah, I guess." That was at least an hour's drive away from our destination and we'd have to cab it there, but if that was our only option...

"Shit, bro, they're saying an hour."

"Goddamn it."

"We can always use the Flint hangar. I parked the Escalade there last month."

I hadn't come this close just to miss seeing her grand opening. Where could I land that wasn't going to take us another hour to get there?

"It's still going to take over an hour."

"Bro, I mean, you can park at Shenandoah Golf Club?" I think Rahim meant it as a joke, but shit, that was an excellent idea.

"Fucking genius."

"I was kidding."

"I know. Doesn't mean that it wasn't perfect." The adrenaline that had been absent for eight months now pumped through my veins.

"At least we're club members." Rahim chuckled.

"Yup, and distant cousins of the officers on the board." I laughed. "Let's land this bad boy."

"What's going on?" Carter came into the cockpit. "Why haven't we landed yet?"

"We're landing now," I said.

He stood over my shoulder. "That's not the Waterford Corporate."

"There is a delay there," I said.

"Did you get clearance somewhere else?" Carter asked.

"Sort of."

"Bro, we are going to land at Shenandoah."

"The fucking golf club?"

"Yup."

"Well, shit." Carter laughed as he headed back out of the cockpit. "Hey, Perky, you thought since we got married things got boring? Well, tonight, the West Bloomfield Police might just arrest us."

I ignored his amusement and concentrated on landing. The golf course was in view, and I shot up a little prayer to anyone that might be listening. *Please don't let me get arrested before I get a chance to see Summer.*

As we touched ground, relief washed over me, and I sat back in my chair to steady my heartbeat. Fuck, I couldn't believe I'd just landed on a golf course. I was going to have to gift a very large donation to the Chaldean Culture Center and the golf course, cover the cost for fixing the grass, and whatever else they wanted.

"Bro."

"I know."

"I can't believe that just happened."

"Let's do this." I undid my seatbelt and headed out of

the cockpit to find Kendall and Carter looking out the window of the plane.

"Everyone is coming out to see what's going on," Kendall said.

"I think I hear sirens too," Carter said.

"Shit," Rahim said.

"It's okay, I got this. I'll tell them that I was having contractions." Kendall put her hands over her round belly. "And that we needed an emergency landing."

"Are you sure?" I said.

"Yes, you go. We got this."

"Okay, tell the manager that I'll pay for all the damages tomorrow morning."

I opened the hatch to the airplane and nearly laughed when Carter shouted, "We need a doctor! Help, doctor!"

I eased away in the midst of people walking out of the ballroom to see what was going on. People had their phones, taking pictures and videos. A bride and groom were in the middle of a picture session on the golf course. Guilt washed over me for ruining their wedding photos.

"Hey, there's a plane back there. You're welcome to take pictures in it or whatever you want. Tell the two guys that Nas said it's okay."

"Cool, thanks." The photographer, a young guy with black-rimmed glasses and black spiky hair fist-bumped me. "That's going to make the pictures badass."

With a "no problem" and a "sorry, hope I didn't ruin your wedding" to the awestricken couple, I found the nearest golf cart and took off the two miles to my girl's restaurant. I only hoped all this wasn't in vain.

CHAPTER 17

This was what thirty looked like, and it was wonderful. The sight of all my friends and family in my restaurant, enjoying my food and celebrating with me, made my heart soar. But something was still missing. A part of me was still not complete.

"These bureks are delicious. Better than Nana's." My cousin Rita took another bite of the Middle Eastern eggroll. "And the way it crunches in my mouth." She actually moaned.

"And the potato chop... How can something be so flaky, buttery, and crispy all at once?" Sandy, Rita's sister, took another bite and swooned. "Seriously, don't let Nana hear us."

Rita and Sandy were sisters but couldn't look further apart. While Rita had the same dark brown hair and eyes as mine, Sandy was a freckled redhead with hazel eyes she'd inherited from her father's side.

With muffled giggles, all three of us looked wildly around the room to be sure we weren't overheard, because if my paternal grandmother heard anyone even hint that my cooking was better, the whole restaurant would be schooled. In truth, I owed my nana for my passion for Middle Eastern cuisine because she was my first teacher—my mother can hardly boil water—and I'd refined the techniques she taught me in culinary school while I learned and developed my own culinary perspective.

The reviews were great so far, and I'd asked everyone to be completely honest about the menu because no one tells you the truth like family. I'd worked really hard on this menu. I wanted it to be filled with our traditional dishes and a nod to my heritage but still add a bit of flair to allow my training to shine through. In addition to my own take on my nana's bureks, potato chop, arook, mini kibbee bites, and meat pies, I also included beef tips and lamb ribs infused with a very special lemony garlic sauce. The appetizers were all served family-style, and I might have gone a little overboard with Middle Eastern salads, like fattoush and tabouleh, and a Spanish arugula salad with walnuts, cranberries, and feta. Of course, I had to add dips to accompany the salads, like hummus and baba ghanoush.

"I'm so stuffed." Sandy leaned back in her chair. "I need a break."

"Well, save some room. You have to taste my chicken cream chop—it's the next course." I grinned.

"I think it's time for your speech." Camille tapped me on the shoulder. I hated public speaking, so she knew I needed someone to make me do it when it was time. I sighed and downed the rest of my wine.

"There you go, a little liquid courage."

"Do I look okay?" I fixed the beautiful red form-fitting dress Sara had brought me and adjusted the cleavage that spilled out a little too much for a family gathering.

"You look absolutely fuckable," Camille whispered while she leaned in and pretended to be fixing the off-the-shoulder strap. Knowing full well that it would make me laugh and loosen me up before I got up onstage.

"I don't think my rabbit cares what I'm wearing," I whispered back.

"You never know." She laughed.

I made my way to the DJ. He was spinning an old-school Arabic song I was sure my cousins had requested because of the way they were singing and swaying their hips to the music.

"What's good, birthday girl? Ready for the welcome speech?"

"Yeah, I think."

"You'll be fine. Just speak from the heart. These are your people."

I gave him a small smile and nodded. I was ready. These were my people, my family and friends, everyone I cared about. Well, almost everyone.

"All right, let's give it up for the lady of the night, our birthday girl and owner of this rocking joint right here, Ms. Summer Seba."

Everyone was super sweet with their applause. They cheered and whistled, and even gave me a really loud *halhula*. It eased whatever stage fright I had tonight.

"Thank you, Sal. Let's give it up for DJ Sal for his fine tunes." I clapped, and everyone joined me in a round of applause for the DJ.

"I want to officially welcome you to Sweet Pea. This place, this very building, down to the name of the restaurant, has been my dream ever since I was in high school. And I can't believe that I'm standing here right now. This has been the most incredible and challenging eight months of my life. I'm so grateful to have you all here to share it with me. " Another round of applause and cheers made me laugh, and I had to talk over them to get them to listen. "Okay, *yella*, let me finish, so we can get to the dinner." Someone shouted something about wanting to get to the sweet table, and there were a few murmurs about being too full for more food, earning more approvals and chuckles from the crowd.

"I want to do some shout-outs. To my parents for always believing in me and encouraging me to follow my dreams, even when I didn't realize that was what you were doing." That earned me a few more chuckles, and I could have sworn my mother was saying something like, "She's right, that girl is always taking what I say wrong."

"My siblings, Sara and George. Thanks for being my food tasters for the past twenty years, my partners in crime, always cheering me on, and of course, making me an awesome auntie." That earned a little cheering from my nieces and nephews.

"Does this mean you won't deliver food to my house anymore?" George shouted.

"You can work out a deal for deliveries," I assured him.

"Nana, you were my first cooking teacher, and I wouldn't be standing here today if it wasn't for the wonderful recipes you passed down to me. I love you, Nana."

My grandmother beamed with pride and wiped a tear from her rosy cheek.

"To my dear friend, Camille, thank you for being by my side through this whole experience." She knew I was talking about Naseem as well as the restaurant, but no one but my mom and Sara knew the complete truth to that story.

She lifted her glass in a salute to me, and Sal handed me another wine glass.

"And to you all, my wonderful, loving family. Thank you all for being here and for all the love and support you've shown me tonight. I love you all so very much. Now, eat up. We have lots of food and to-go containers. I might have made a little extra so y'all don't have to cook tomorrow."

That earned me some more shouts of joy.

"Cheers." I lifted my glass in salute, and everyone mimicked me before I took a swig out of my drink.

"Now, I'll hand you back over to DJ Sal to get this party rolling." I handed the microphone back to Sal and started to head toward the kitchen to check in on my kitchen staff.

"Why did you name the restaurant Sweet Pea?"

That raspy drawl nearly made me drop the glass from between my fingertips. I halted midstep but didn't have the courage to turn around. What if I'd imagined his voice? What if I'd wanted to hear it so badly I'd hallucinated it?

"Look at me, please, Summer." The plea in his voice was enough to break me, but instead, I closed my eyes and counted to five before facing him. I needed composure, even though every ounce in my body throbbed at just the sound of his voice. But what I saw when our gazes met broke my heart. He'd lost weight, he'd grown a beard, and his eyes seemed like he hadn't slept in months.

She was counting—I just knew it—but her time was up, and I wasn't leaving here without an answer. I'd walked in just as she'd taken the mic, and I was able to watch her uninterrupted for at least a few minutes. I missed her face, those all-knowing big brown eyes that haunted my dreams, and that delicious mouth. My body ached to wrap my arms around her waist and pull her against me. I missed her scent and the way her breath hitched right before she laughed.

But when her eyes found mine, I didn't find the same excitement that radiated through my body. Her expression fell and she recoiled. My heart sank, and I started to back away from her. I couldn't handle another rejection from her.

"Wait."

Like a trained pup, I halted at her command, even though I knew she wasn't happy to see me.

"I thought you wanted to know why I named my restaurant Sweet Pea."

"Yeah." I kept my back to her and my eyes glued to the floor.

"I named it Sweet Pea as a message to the love of my life."

For a moment, I couldn't respond. It took a moment for my heart and mind to catch up with each other. I turned to face her. Her eyes sparkled with pleasure, and that gave me hope to continue.

"What's the message?" I breathed.

"I will always and forever be his sweet pea."

She closed the space between us. My pulse quickened. Her hand touched my face, and I melted into her touch.

"I should never have walked away from you in

Argentina. I'm so sorry. I believed walking away from each other was best because I assumed having the power to hurt each other was something we could fix by being apart. But I was wrong. It physically hurts to be apart."

"Summer, before Rio, I pictured life in terms of the next party, the next test against my immortality. I kept flying the world, looking for somewhere I belonged, but nowhere felt like home until I reconnected with you. A fucking forest with snakes and bugs in Rio felt like coming home because I was with you. I fucking love you, Summer. Fucking put me out of my misery. Marry me, be the mother of my children. Start a life—"

She grabbed my face in her hands, and her stare burned down to my soul. "Yes. A thousand times, yes."

Finally, her lips touched mine for a brief moment, and for the first time in eight months, everything was right in my world.

"Bro, finally. Maybe now he won't be such a bitch at work." I turned to see Rahim, Camille, Carter, and Kendall, all standing behind us, grinning like idiots. I kept Summer tight against me and faced my friends.

"How did you get away from the cops?" I asked.

"Cops? What cops?" Summer started to freak out.

"Bro, it's fine, no worries. But we were lucky. When Carter started shouting for a doctor, Nash showed up."

"Nash? Here? I didn't even know he was coming to Michigan. Didn't we take him to California last week?"

"He was there for the wedding we crashed. He took a commercial flight from Cali." He pointed behind him, and I saw my brother shaking hands with George.

He pretended to give Kendall a checkup, called it a false alarm, and drove us here. But you are going to have some major explaining to do at the club."

"Wait, are you guys saying you landed the plane at Shenandoah Golf Club?"

"Yes." We all laughed at Summer's bemused expression.

"Oh, shit. Here's my mom," Summer said.

"Your mom used to love me."

"That was before you broke her daughter's heart, twice," Camille said.

"Oh, and she's bringing my dad." Summer nervously laughed. "I think I see a shotgun wedding in the near future."

"No shotgun required, I've already proposed again."

"You proposed to my daughter without asking me for my permission?" Summer's dad looked exactly like he did in the picture Summer showed me of him with the grandchildren. He was a short, stocky man, with a balding head and stern brown eyes.

He always had this way about him that scared the hell out of me. "No, sir. Well, yes, sir, I mean *Amo*." I used the proper greeting for an elder Chaldean man because I came to my senses. "I'm sorry. I just wanted to make sure she still didn't hate me before I asked for your permission."

He laughed. "I always liked you. You were a good boy from a good family. God bless your parents in Heaven."

"Thank you, *Amo*." At his words, pain rumbled my chest. I avoided family and my culture so much, I believed for this reason. Being around them made me miss my parents more.

"So, can I marry your daughter?"

He glanced at Mrs. Seba, who made a show as she pondered my question. She was an attractive older woman with short dark hair and eyes just like Summer's.

"Yes, you have our blessing. But if you break my daughter's heart again, I will have someone dump your body in the Detroit River."

"He is kidding." Mrs. Seba's warm palm cupped my face in the way my mother used to when she was proud. "Only a little bit."

"Welcome to the family, son."

Mr. Seba shook my hand with a firm grip and pulled me into a manly bear hug in the same kind of embrace my father used to give me. Warm, strong, and fatherly.

CHAPTER 18

"Can I have your attention, everyone?" My father's voice caught me off guard. He'd taken center stage beside DJ Sal and the murmured laughter subsided in the restaurant. My father had a charisma that always commanded respect, but it was the joy he always exuded that made everyone stop and listen when he spoke.

I glanced at my Naseem, and he beamed back at me. His strong hand wrapped around mine beneath the table, and warmth wrapped around my heart, healing the broken pieces with his touch and presence.

"*Shukeren.*" My dad gave his thanks in Arabic and smiled warmly at the crowd. "It gives me such joy to see us all together, celebrating my youngest girl and all her accomplishments, but it looks like we have more to celebrate tonight."

My father's stare locked with mine, and my heart swelled from the delight in his gaze. "You might have noticed there is a gentleman, Naseem Kakos, son of the late Nabil and Theresa Kakos, seated beside my daughter, and you know we have rules—there's no boyfriends or girlfriends allowed at family events."

"Should we take him outside, *Amu*?" my cousin Omar asked, earning a few cheers and laughs from everyone.

"No, that won't be necessary." My father smirked. "You see, this young man has asked to marry Summer, and her mother and I have given our blessings."

A sequence of cheers erupted around the room.

"Welcome, Naseem. Do you play football? It is a requirement for the men in our family."

Naseem's hand tightened within mine, and for a moment, I feared this was all a little too much for him, a little too fast because we'd just connected again. But one look into the happiness in his face washed away my worries.

"Yes, *Amu*." Naseem laughed.

"Okay, one more toast." My father lifted his glass in salute. "To Naseem and Summer, may God always bless and protect you."

Naseem and I were swarmed from all sides with eager force, and we separated while everyone gave us their heartfelt well wishes and blessings. I noticed my brother hadn't approached, and even though he'd pulled a chair for Nash at his table, he didn't give us congratulations of his own when Nash approached.

"You know, I always knew that you would find your way back together. I couldn't picture anyone else as my sister."

"Well, I'm glad you had faith in us," I whispered. "We sure didn't."

Nash was almost a carbon copy of Naseem but didn't have the broad and muscular body, and instead of dark-as-night eyes, Nash had inherited his mother's whiskey-colored eyes.

"I'm just happy Carter and Rahim convinced him to come. He has been hell since Rio."

I watched while my male cousins surrounded Naseem, and he was holding his own with them, but my brother was nowhere in sight. Dread gripped my chest. "What about George? Is he okay with this?"

Nash patted my shoulder and smiled. "George has always had his own way of doing things." With one last hug, Nash walked away, and a swarm of girl cousins circled me.

For the rest of the night, Naseem and I didn't have a moment alone. Between keeping an eye on things in the kitchen, entertaining family, and getting dragged onto the dance floor for a little line dancing, the entire night was a blur of laughter and excitement. While people were gathering their things and saying their goodbyes, Naseem placed his hand on the small of my back and seared my skin beneath my dress.

"I'm dying to kiss you." His warm breath teased my ear, and my body burned.

"Me too." My face probably matched my red dress.

"How long do you think you can sneak away?" His five o'clock shadow tickled my bare shoulder, leaving trembles in its wake.

"I could spare an hour or two." Our eyes met, and fire glazed in his stare. "What do you have in mind?"

"Got a threatening call." He smirked. "I need to move my plane, and I figured you might want to fly with me."

My heart did a little cheer at the warmth in his eyes, and I trembled with need for this man. I couldn't believe he was still here. That we were getting married, and my whole family had met him. I should have pinched myself, but I feared waking up and finding this was all just a dream.

"Will I finally get to be part of that club?" I tugged at his black tie.

He licked his lips. "Absolutely."

A voice cleared, and Naseem's tie dropped from my fingertips. There was no way anyone knew what we were talking about, but I'm sure our body language told a story of its own. George—also known as Vin Diesel because he could pass as his stunt double—stared at us with disapproval, and my heart fell. I wasn't going to let him say something to ruin this for me, but I couldn't seem to find my words. My sister-in-law, Renee, stood behind George with uneasiness in her hazel eyes. She intertwined the ends of her highlighted blond hair between her fingertips in a constant motion—it was her tell, something she'd done since high school when she was anxious.

George took a calculated step toward Naseem and pinned him with his glare.

Naseem didn't speak, but he didn't back down either. He lifted his chin, and his stare met my brother's while the hand on the small of my back wrapped around my waist, claiming me. Something in their body language told me that I should let them handle it, but it didn't ease the lump in my throat. My brother's approval was just as important to me as my parents'.

"You made a vow to me a long time ago." George's glower never wavered from Naseem's face. My stomach knotted and my mouth went dry. What vow? What was I missing? I looked from Naseem to George, trying to assess if I needed to holler for reinforcements. Naseem's cool and calm presence and his firm grip on my waist kept me from losing my own composure.

"You broke it." George took one step closer and I held my breath. "Why?"

"After my dad..." Naseem paused. "I didn't know how to try."

My heart cried from the sadness in his tone, and I wanted to kick George for putting it there.

"And now?"

"I'm still not good enough." Naseem looked down on me, and a sweet smile relaxed on his lips. "But until my last breath, I will do everything in my power to make her as happy she makes me."

My heart swelled ten times its size and tears stung my eyes.

"Right answer." Beaming, George clasped hands with Naseem and did that manly one-handed hug. "That's a good thing too, because *Baba* said something about the Detroit River, if not."

George's stare met mine and affection radiated from his face. "You are going to make a beautiful bride."

I wrapped my arms around his neck. "I love you."

He squeezed me tighter. "Love you too, sis."

With one last glance at Naseem, George clasped hands with Renee and headed to the exit.

"What the heck was that about? What vow?" I whispered.

"That's between me and my new brother."

~

HAD I REALLY LANDED THE PLANE ON A GOLF COURSE, stolen a golf cart, and raced to Sweet Pea like a bat out of hell? The cool night air swirled around us, Summer's floral scent kissed my senses, and serenity enveloped me. Finally, at the door of my plane, I hurried to release the hatch and stairs. I was desperate to hold Summer and touch her—reassure myself that all this wasn't just another dream. That I wasn't going to wake up in my bed in Boston alone, lonely and completely miserable.

"So, this is Jade?"

"Nope. This beauty is the newest member of Fly Kakos." I led my girl onto the plane and sealed the flap shut.

"It's beautiful." Summer ran her fingers against the soft leather seat beside her, a sweet smile playing on her lips.

"Yeah, she's a stunner, just like her namesake."

"You named her after someone?"

"Yup."

"Really, who?"

"You." I closed the space between us. "I named her Summer, after you."

"Me?" Bewilderment danced in her eyes. "Even after the way I walked away from you? I've regretted my actions every day. You came to me, offered me everything, and I still let you believe that I married someone else." Tears streamed from her eyes. "I was such a fool."

I pulled her body against mine. "It's okay, sweet pea, it's okay."

"Why aren't you angry with me?" she whispered.

I tilted her face to look at me, her soft brown eyes filled with gut-wrenching guilt. "I'm happy that all that crap is behind us and you're with me now."

"I love you." She kissed my lips, and I melted into her embrace. Her fingers tugged on my hair, pulling me closer, firmer against her frame. My body pulsed with growing need.

"I love you, forever." I teased her lips with my tongue "Come on, I want to show you my cock"—I paused and nibbled her neck in that spot that always seemed to make her putty in my hands—"pit."

Her lighthearted laugh was heaven to my ears as she followed me into the cockpit. I took my seat and radioed in to the Flint Airport and was pleased to finally have clearance to land.

Summer sat cross-legged in the copilot seat beside me while I readied for takeoff, and in a matter of moments, we were in the air. Tonight, with her beside me, I buzzed with excitement.

"So, how do I join that club you mentioned? She kicked off her heels and unzipped her dress from a side panel along the curve of her body. The dress opened, exposing her creamy skin, but she took it a step further, shimmying it all the way off her body and onto the cockpit floor.

Her bra was next, and it landed beside her dress. Her tits high, her nipples hard—she rubbed her hands over each with her wicked gaze on me. Her hands traveled down her body to the lace trim of her panties.

"Fuck." I hit the autopilot button. "Take off your panties. We only have about twenty minutes."

"Yes, Captain."

The little strap of black lace landed beside the rest of her clothing, and her doe-eyed stare found mine. "Now what, Captain?"

"Kiss me."

A sweet smile tugged at her lips while she made her way over to my seat and placed her mouth against mine. I loved how confident she was in her own skin. Her self-assurance made her even more desirable to me. Her fingers untied my necktie and unbuttoned my shirt while I undid my belt and zipper.

With a groan, I checked the plane's dashboard to confirm all was still clear and moved my chair back to make a little extra room. I slid my fingers between her legs. Her hips moved to the motion of my hands, and her fingernails dug into my shoulders.

"I need more. I need you." Her greedy hands caressed my cock, and heat covered my skin.

"It's a good thing that Rahim gave me condoms." I reached into my pocket and pulled out the handful he'd slipped me before he and Camille had left the party.

"Remind me to thank him when I see him." She caressed up and down my shaft before placing the condom on me.

"Come here."

My body quaked from the sensation of her naked skin against my own. Her smooth back pressed against my chest, and her sexy ass teased my cock. I'd imagined this so many times, and now that it was real, I was near combustion from sheer anticipation. I ran my hands down her smooth collarbone to her lush tits, and she trembled against me.

"Hold the armrests and lift that sexy ass."

Summer welcomed me inside her sweet warmth. Her whimpers were music to my ears. Her frame rocked up and down my shaft in a slow and sensual movement, driving me senseless.

"Fuck." I examined the instrument panel, and we still had a few minutes before I had to call the tower.

Her seductive figure moved up and down my length—

a slow and steady rhythm of lovemaking. Our bodies danced and delighted in each other. I clasped her hips and controlled her movements, speeding the pace. I imagined being bare inside that sweet, wet pussy, coming inside her, filling her with my seed, and making her the mother of my children. Those thoughts alone were enough to make me explode—but an image of her with a round belly like Kendall's slammed into me.

"Naseem." Her orgasm, along with my name on her lips, was my undoing. Her body quaked on top of me. I savored the sensation of her muscles contracting around me while my release took me.

The city and the runway were coming into view, and I radioed the tower.

"Fly Kakos 007 cleared to land, runway one-eight."

"Cleared to land one-eight, Fly Kakos 007."

Flipping off the autopilot button and preparing for landing, I clasped the yoke and eased it forward.

"We're landing?" Summer panted. "Should I move?"

I kissed her shoulder blade. "No."

The plane shuddered as we lowered over the runway, and my pulse sprinted at the *clank* of the wheels touching down.

"Did that actually just happen?" Summer breathed.

"Did you like it?" I kissed her cheek, already hardening again beneath her.

"Can we do it again?"

"Anytime you want."

After pulling into the hangar, I shifted her body to face me. "I have something for you."

Her fingers teased my cheek and lingered on my lips. "Yeah, what's that?"

I unclasped the chain that held my father's cross and my mother's ring. "I want you to have this."

"Your mom's wedding band?"

"Yeah." My mouth was dry.

"It's beautiful."

"I mean, I'll still get you your own engagement ring and matching band, but I thought...never mind."

I attempted to reclasp the chain, but she stilled my hands and held my face between her delicate fingers. "I love it." She stuck out her left hand. "Put it on me."

"You still want to marry me?"

"Yes, absolutely, I do."

I slid the diamond wedding band on her ring finger, and while I stared into the eyes of the love of my life, the girl who had enthralled me since I was a boy, peace settled in my chest.

I was finally home.

EPILOGUE

Nine Years and Three Months Later

"Happy birthday." I ran my fingers over his hard length through the little access hole of his boxers and admired the soft, velvety skin. "Ready for your fortieth birthday BJ?"

"Fuck." Naseem arched his hips forward. "Yes."

"Eager, huh?" I laughed.

"I'm always eager if it's sex and you."

He helped me ease his boxers below his hips, and his erection greeted me, tall, thick, and strong, waiting for my next move. He put his arms behind his back and watched with appreciation while I moved my hands up and down his length.

"Do you remember the first time I gave you a blowjob?" I licked the head of his sex, and my tongue traveled his length.

"Sophomore year," he hissed. "You were wearing my jersey and nothing else."

"I love how you remember everything."

His eyes watched me like he'd never seen me undress. After nearly ten years of marriage, I never tired of the devotion in his eyes. I undid the tie on my robe and let it fall onto the bed to expose the T-shirt I'd worn underneath. I did a little shimmy to show him the "Kakos" on the back.

"That's my jersey?"

"Yup. It's a little shorter than I remembered, but yeah."

"Where did you find it?"

"In a box in my parents' attic." I couldn't believe my mother had saved the box in which I'd placed the jersey, along with my high school mementos. "It's a good thing they're pack rats."

"You look even better in it now." His hands caressed my backside. "And you know I love when you don't wear panties."

I spread my legs wider, giving him more access. "Today is about you."

Taking him deep into my mouth, I savored the salty, sweet taste of him. The way his hips moved beneath me. He lovingly caressed my thighs, hips, and my behind—and heat stirred in my core. I yelped from the sting of his hand striking my backside.

"Still have the sexiest ass." His fingers stroked between my legs.

My lips moved steadfastly on his shaft, taking him to the hilt, over and over, until he bucked beneath me. I loved watching him squirm from the pleasure I could give him. I don't know if he realized it, but today was a special birthday day. Ten years ago, he believed he wouldn't make it to forty years of age because he assumed he was doomed to his parents' untimely deaths. But today, I wanted to honor him and show him how much we had to celebrate.

"Sweet pea..." He groaned.

My butt rose from the bed and landed on his chest. I wavered from the brief distraction and lost control of my seduction. Within seconds, I was on all fours and his cock pressed against my thigh. "On my birthday, I want to come inside my wife."

"Yes, please," I whimpered.

If that was what he wanted on his birthday, who was I to argue? I had such a giving husband, and I'd take whatever he wanted to give me. My body was ready for him, and his entry was rough and dominating. I moaned in pure gratification. Heat entwined inside my core and sent tremors throughout my body.

"Fuck, that jersey..." His hand slid beneath and caressed my breasts. "I feel like I'm seventeen again."

His wicked fingers traveled between my legs, caressing and teasing the center of me. He played my body like a master musician. My body pulsated with each stroke.

The bedroom doorknob jittered and rattled. A loud knock came from the other side. My heart sank.

Naseem stilled. "Shit."

"Why is the door locked?" Skylar's annoyed voice came from the other side of the door.

"Mom? Dad? Are you awake?" Logan's voice came next.

"Cock-blockers." I pressed my face into the pillows. "Do you think they'll go away if we don't answer?"

"Mom. Dad?" The door jerked again. "You think we should call the police?"

Skylar's concern was nearly heartbreaking, and had I

not just been a few seconds away from an earth-shattering orgasm, I'd think the whole thing was adorable.

Naseem chuckled. "Does that answer your question?" He eased out of me, and I groaned in frustration.

"Maybe we should call Nana and *Jiddo* before we call the police," Logan said.

"Don't call anyone. I'm coming," I yelled toward the door.

"You were gonna come, really hard." Naseem stepped into his joggers.

I nearly growled with frustration and put on my robe. "I was so close."

"Mom?" Skylar's voice. "Hurry, you're messing up Dad's surprise."

"One second, honey." I reached for the door. "I'd do anything for one day at that waterfall."

"That can be arranged." He smirked. "Still have that hot-pink bikini?"

"Who needs clothes?" I winked.

"You never need them in my company."

I unlocked the door, and before I could even stand back, it burst open.

~

The dynamic duo, our eight-year-old twins, Skylar and Logan, burst through the door, and Summer almost toppled over from the sheer force of the storm. Her cheeks were flushed, her breath a little winded, and her long curls wild and untamed from the lovemaking that had been so rudely interrupted by the munchkins.

"Daddy." Two waist-high bodies collided into me. "Happy birthday."

Scooping them up, I tipped my head back and closed my eyes. I savored the warmth of their little faces pressed on each side of my neck and breathed in the fruity scent of their shampoo. Every time I held them, looked into their little faces, or recognized an inherited trait in them, I was mystified I'd never wanted children. Now, I couldn't imagine life without them. Looking down at my kids, pride swelled in my chest, and a little sadness too. My parents would never get to see them, and my children would never get to meet my parents.

Logan peeked his head up first, and his whiskey-colored eyes just like my mom's and brother's danced with excitement. They were getting too heavy to carry together, and I set them down beside the bed. "Ready to have a family fantastic fun day?"

"What do you monsters have planned?" I tickled his side.

"Mom, what's with your hair?" Skylar, who was an image of Summer, crossed her arms over her chest. "And why aren't you dressed? We have a schedule to keep."

Summer smirked and glanced at me. "I'm sorry honey. My plans got...a little derailed his morning." Translation: *"I was just trying to give your dad his birthday BJ, but he wanted more."* Skylar not only looked like Summer with her dark, curly hair and eyes, but she also had her type-A personality. The eight-year-old was driven by lists, goals, and order. While Logan was more about the adventure, like his old man.

"Okay, why don't you give me and Daddy twenty minutes to get showered and dressed—and you guys make sure everything else stays on schedule downstairs?"

"What's happening downstairs?"

Logan laughed. "We can't tell you, or it won't be a surprise."

The doorbell rang. "Who can that be?" I asked, looking at the time. "It's hardly nine."

"Ugh, they're early, and you're late, Mom," Skylar scolded.

I held back a chuckle and glanced at Summer, who was holding back a giggle of her own.

"Skylar, honey, it's okay. We have plenty of time." The doorbell rang again. "Go get the door, and we'll be down in twenty minutes, okay? Promise."

"I'm going to answer the door." Logan sped out of the room.

"Make sure you check who it is before you open the door," Summer hollered behind him and made her way to the window that faced the driveway.

"Fine, but if you're not downstairs in twenty minutes, I'll be back," Skylar said.

"Yes, ma'am." I kissed her cheek.

"Dad, I just want this to be your best birthday yet." She wiped tears from her eyes.

My heart swelled. "Oh, baby girl, it is as long as I get to spend it with you, Logan, and your mom."

"Okay."

"Now, go make sure your brother didn't let in robbers."

She giggled and ran out of the room.

"Seriously, who are we expecting at nine a.m.?"

Summer laughed. "Oh, you just wait."

She locked the door behind the kids and took off the jersey. "Since we only have twenty minutes, we should shower together to save time." With a wink, she stepped into the bathroom, and I followed that sexy ass into the shower.

After the quickest shower sex and promises of more to come later, we were putting on the last items of clothing when someone knocked on our bedroom door.

"It's time," our little timekeeper hollered.

"On our way." Summer giggled.

She reached out her hand for mine. "Ready?"

"As ready as I'll ever be."

Summer led me down our spiral staircase and the loudest shout of "Surprise!" nearly toppled me off the last step of the stairs. Everyone was gathered in my kitchen—which was decorated with birthday banners, balloons, and a continental breakfast. Hugs, kisses, and greetings from our entire family and closest friends surrounded me.

"Can anyone tell me what the hell is going on?" I shouted over all the chatter and excitement. "I mean, I love you all, but what the hell are you doing here before noon on a Saturday?"

Carter stepped up and handed me a flight plan. "We are going to Rio, brother."

"Hotel Love?" The idea of couples massages and a dip in the hot tub was heaven. Since Sweet Pea was now a chain restaurant with ten different locations across the US, and Fly Kakos had expanded to all fifty states, there hadn't been enough time to get away.

"No, we're going somewhere more family-friendly."

"I can't wait to meet the monkey," Logan said. "I wonder if he'll pee on me."

"Maria Rosa's villa?" I asked.

"No, mine. She sold it to me last month."

"Well, shit. When do we leave?"

"Rahim is already at Fly Kakos Detroit. We take off in an hour and a half."

"We're already packed, Dad." Skylar and Logan rolled out suitcases from the laundry room.

"Well, we better get to the airport, huh?" I smiled at my planner girl and kissed my wife on the forehead.

While everyone buzzed around to get the kitchen cleaned up and to get ready to go, I pulled Summer into the laundry room and closed the door. "You keep surprising me, sweet pea."

"Is that a good thing?" Her soft lips caressed mine in a chaste kiss.

"It's one of the many things I adore about you."

"Good, because I reserved us two nights at a resort. George and Renee are taking the kids for us."

She placed another hurried kiss on my lips and attempted to pull away, but I held her tight against me. "Fuck, I'm forty today."

She smoothed the material over my chest. "How does it feel?"

I slipped my hands down to her ass over her jeans. "It feels fucking fantastic." I'd once feared to even dream about a life and family with Summer because I was so frightened of my own mortality. Feared dying young and leaving my family behind in the way my parents left Nash and me. But looking back, all the happiness we'd shared these nine years would have never been if I hadn't gotten my head out of my ass and realized how stupid I'd been.

"Even with all the kids and family everywhere?"

"Better because of it." I consumed her mouth and pressed her against the door with my own. She moaned against my lips.

"Mom." The door jolted.

Summer sighed. "One sec, helping Daddy get something from the laundry."

Skylar called, "Why do you keep locking the doors today?"

Carter's laugh echoed from outside the door. "Skylar, honey, can you please make sure Uncle George takes all your suitcases to the car?"

"Two days in a hotel, no kids," Summer whispered against my lips.

"I can't fucking wait." I pressed my lips against hers once more. "I love you."

"I love you too."

Want to keep up with all of the new releases in Vi Keeland and Penelope Ward's Cocky Hero Club world? Make sure you sign up for the official Cocky Hero Club newsletter for all the latest on our upcoming books:

https://www.subscribepage.com/CockyHeroClub

Check out other books in the Cocky Hero Club series:
http://www.cockyheroclub.com

ACKNOWLEDGMENTS

To Vi and Penelope, thank you for inviting me to join the Cocky Hero Club. I'm so happy to be part of the CHC author family and truly appreciate the opportunity. Thank you, Dan, for being so kind and helpful during the entire publishing process.

To my cover designer, A.J. Norris, at Delicious Nights Designs, thank you for making my cover so freaking sexy! I really appreciate all the time and effort you spent on finding the perfect model for my story.

To my editor, Jennifer Miller, words can't describe how grateful I am for all your hard work in making my story shine. It seemed like kismet when I learned you knew about flying. Thank you for being so kind and taking me on last minute. You are a true rock star!

To Jennifer Eaton, thank you for your formatting magic and making my document storybook ready.

To my Golden Girls – Amalie, Aliza, MK, Shaila and Sienna. You ladies are my rock, my sounding board, and my cheerleaders. I couldn't have made it through last year without you. I will forever be grateful for your love, support, and dirty jokes. Love you ladies!

To the CHC readers, thank you for giving my story a chance. I hope you love Naseem and Summer's story as much as I do.

ABOUT THE AUTHOR

Sage Spelling's love affair with romance started when she was a child and her mother told tall tales of faraway worlds filled with magic, mystery and happy endings. Whatever hardship the characters suffered, in the end they were granted a happily ever after. It was guaranteed and she knew her investment in the characters and the story was going to be rewarded. Growing up in a strict Chaldean Catholic family, she found freedom in-between the pages of a novel. While she read, she wasn't confined to her family's rules and principles. She could be anyone . . . anywhere. Sage is a Potter-head, Supernatural fanatic, BDB Harlot, a Fashionista and a believer in love at first sight.

Follow Sage Spelling's journey at https://sagespelling.com/